BELLA BRIGHT
AND THE
GHOST
GAME

BELLA BRIGHT
AND THE
GHOST
GAME

CAROLYN WARD
ILLUSTRATED BY BEATRIZ CASTRO

WELBECK
FLAME

Published in 2023 by Welbeck Flame
An imprint of Welbeck Children's Limited,
part of Welbeck Publishing Group.
Offices in: London - 20 Mortimer Street, London W1T 3JW &
Sydney - Level 17, 207 Kent St, Sydney NSW 2000 Australia

www.welbeckpublishing.com

Design and layout © Welbeck Children's Limited 2023

Text copyright © Carolyn Ward, 2023
Illustrations copyright © Beatriz Castro, 2023

A CIP catalogue record for this book is available from the British Library.

ISBN: 978 1 80130 095-7

Printed and bound by CPI Group (UK)

10 9 8 7 6 5 4 3 2 1

IN MEMORY OF MY BELOVED DAD,
JAMES FINNEY.

FOR MY BRILLIANT AND BRAVE MUM,
ELIZABETH FINNEY.

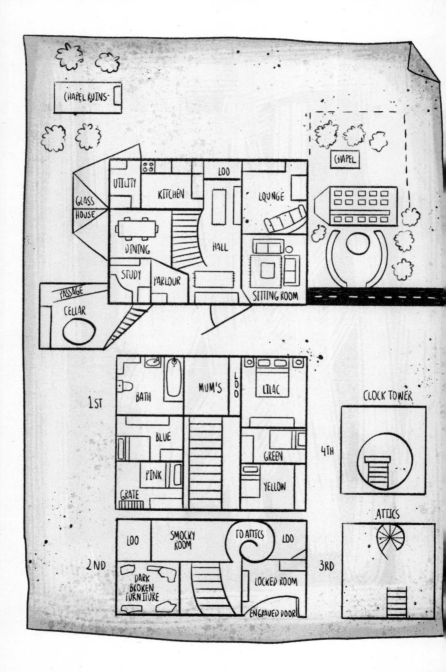

'We're here!'

Mum's voice cut through the podcast burbling from my headphones and I pushed them back, sitting up and looking out of the car window. In front of us was our new home: Darkling Manor.

Mum turned up the long winding drive, and I swear a flock of bats took off from the roof. I leaned forwards, not quite believing my eyes. It looked like a haunted house, all black and gnarly and wonky. I saw it had a clock tower in the centre, and about fourteen crazily angled chimneys. Mum was oohing and ahhing but I just shook my head.

She drove all the way up and jerked to a halt

by the front door, where there was an overgrown turning circle for visitors to take one look and keep going.

We climbed out of the car and I had a babyish urge to hold her hand. Instead, I folded my arms, scowling. The sun was going down behind the house, casting a blood-red edge around the coppery roof tiles, which glowed as if they were on fire. I fiddled with my phone, all of my senses on high alert. The neighbourhood was quiet except for the mad flapping of a crow, and the growl of an occasional passing car.

'Are you sure about this, Mum?' I asked, absorbing the state of the place.

'Of course, Bells!' She put one arm around my shoulders and squeezed me tight. 'Another absolute gem for our portfolio! Just imagine what we can do to it!'

Probably best to just demolish it and start again, I thought, resting my head on her shoulder for a moment.

2

Mum fished in her massive handbag for Darkling's keys, which the owner had posted to her last week. There were loads of them on a metal ring big enough for me to slip my hand in.

'Couldn't lose these,' joked Mum, trying to keep it all light-hearted despite the nightmare we were walking into. She struggled to wind one of the biggest keys off for me. I looked down at it, flakes of rust already staining my hand orange. The properties we did up always started off rough, but once we got a team of builders, carpenters, carpet-fitters, electricians, plumbers and the random odd-job people, they ended up looking amazing. Mrs Hallorann was Darkling's owner, and had inspected Mum's work at the old water mill we'd just finished, saying she was 'blown away'! She was American and liked wearing a feathery wrap. Combined with her long, skinny legs, she reminded me of an ostrich.

Mum slotted her key into the huge, arched front door as I tripped up the crooked step.

3

After a good deal of wrenching and clanking, the door swung wide with a sharp creak. It seemed to fall open at a downward angle, too, like the house behind it had sunk.

'Have the surveyors checked this place out?' I asked. Mum usually insisted on her surveyor, a yellow-eyed old man called Bob, to thoroughly check anywhere we would be living. He followed us all over, happy enough as Mum paid for his train tickets. Before Bob she had fallen through a floor, and did not want it to happen again.

'Actually... no.' She looked back at me guiltily, swiping black curls out of her eyes. 'There wasn't time with this one, as Mrs H wanted the work starting straight away. It's to be a hotel, did I tell you?'

I nodded. There was an odd breeze flowing out of the doorway at us, like the house was exhaling. It smelled like I imagined a grave would, after a hundred years of rotting dampness. I wrinkled my nose.

Mum went in, stumbling a little on the floor, which was tiled like a checkerboard in a way that made me blink. I stumbled too, and had to force my attention away from the mesmerising patterns.

'Mrs H wants everything.' Mum sounded gleeful as she stared around. The ceiling was high, with a whole extra layer of dust-filled cobwebs hanging from it like a thousand tiny hammocks. 'Complete revamp, all the furniture, fixtures and fittings. This will be such fun, Bella!'

The house certainly looked like a lot of things, but fun was not one of them. I opened my mouth to disagree, when the front door slammed behind us.

'Bella!' tutted Mum, examining an old cracked mirror. 'Don't slam doors in old properties!'

'I didn't!' I held my hands out and stared pointedly back at the door. Couldn't she see I was miles away from the thing?

'I need you to be careful, OK?' she called back at me as she went into the room on the right, while I pulled a face. I had been nowhere near the stupid door.

I turned back to it, as now her key was on the outside and I didn't fancy any local jokers locking us in. The handle stuck, and took ages of wrenching and yanking before it suddenly swung down at me, making me stagger. I clambered back up like some sort of ice-skating giraffe and snatched the key from the outside, kicking the thing shut again. But now, of course, the door wouldn't fit into the frame.

'What?' I muttered.

Finally I got it closed, by jumping up and down and using my left shoulder. I put our keys on the floor by a vase shaped like a screaming woman. Who'd left that there? I set off to follow Mum, when I heard a piano playing. I faltered, listening. Whoever it was wasn't very good. They were playing scales, running up and down in pitch, but getting more than a couple wrong.

'Where's the piano?' I called out.

'Piano? There isn't one of those here. Anything valuable got taken out by the last owners.'

I screwed up my face. No piano? The quiet tinkling stopped, and I swore I heard a giggle.

'Mum, is there someone here?' I called again, looking around me just in case there was a squatter or burglar or something.

'Nope – nobody's been in here for months.' Mum breezed out of one door and flashed a grin at me. I swallowed.

Then something totally bonkers happened.

There was a whisper in my ear.

I froze, standing absolutely rigid. Everything else in the house was now so silent I could hear my heart thumping. The whisper made my ear cold, like a snake tongue tickling deep inside my head. I started to shake and, after a moment, forced my feet to move, running as fast as I could after Mum.

I risked a glance back along the hallway, trying to pull in a breath. There was definitely nobody here except for Mum and me. This was impossible. I rubbed my ear, trying to lose the feeling.

I managed not to whimper as I scampered through the front parlour after her, my mind trying to explain what I'd heard. It didn't make any sense at all.

Three words. With another of those giggles.

They ran on a loop through my head.

'Play my game!'

2

I ran my hand along the red metal gates that seemed to be exactly the same as the metal gates wrapping around every school I'd ever been to, and took a deep breath. I'd managed to get some sleep in our first night at Darkling, even though I had insisted on sharing a room with Mum and she snored like a gorilla.

'You could have that super little pink room by the stairs?' she'd wheedled, but I shook my head hard enough to make my plaits fly into my mouth. No way was I sleeping alone in this place until we'd hoovered… I mean, all of those cobwebs! Clearly there would be a million giant spiders just waiting for me to fall asleep so they could

9

crawl over my face. The misbehaving front door, the piano... and the whispering... no *way*.

I kept thinking about it, that voice. It had sounded quite young. Maybe there was a kid who had sneaked in. Old properties always had unlocked doorways and passages and kitchen gardens, and sometimes we'd had trouble with local teenagers breaking in to mess about in the grounds of some of the previous places. Mum usually solved it by fitting security lights and beefing up the perimeter fences. I decided to tell her to make it a priority after school. After *school*! I couldn't wait for this day to be over. I had begged Mum to let me stay home and help her with the planning, but she just gave me a massive hug.

'If you don't go to school you won't qualify as an architect or a builder... or a plumber or something useful to our family business.'

She was right, of course. But starting a new school every six to eighteen months was like living in a weird *Groundhog* nightmare.

This school was tall and thin, towering above me, bits of rubbish blowing about in the wind. Counting in my head, I realised Springhill Comprehensive was my eighth school, but it was different in one major way – it was my first secondary school. I was extra-nervous because of this. Due to a very overdue finish on the water mill and the difference between Welsh and English school dates, it meant that I was quite late for the autumn term. Being the new girl nearly two whole *months* after everyone else had already started sucked. Even the fact that it was a Tuesday and not a Monday made it suck BIG TIME. And I was *late*. Off the scale of suck, like a vacuum cleaner on warp speed.

Typical Mum getting busy on a conference call just when I should have been setting off. I was in the background pulling faces to try and get her attention, but all she did was put her hand over the phone and holler 'Remember your speech therapy training!' at me. I opened my mouth to reply but she blew me a kiss and started striding around the drive, yapping about gargoyles, waving to me and sticking her thumb up. I knew I had no chance. Instead of the lift she'd promised me, I had to walk, waiting until I was outside Darkling so my phone actually worked to give me directions. Another thing to remember to tell Mum... get the internet people around to boost the signal. I needed a working phone to do all the normal teenage stuff, like text people and take selfies to spruce up with cat ears. I pulled a face. Who was I kidding? I had never texted anyone except Mum in my life.

Sure, people had been 'friendly' to me at the other schools, but never enough to swap mobile phone numbers. Never enough to get asked around to tea, or gossip about other people. Never. Maybe one good thing about moving house every six-to-eighteen months was the fact that I kept getting new chances. Maybe this time I'd do better.

As I headed in, I couldn't help but think that compared to the other seven schools I'd attended,

Springhill seemed particularly scruffy. There was chipped paint everywhere and black marks on the staircase to my left. The place smelled of dust and hot custard. The skirting boards were mismatched and rough. I diagnosed a little hand-sanding and then some ice-white gloss. As I pushed open about a hundred heavy glass doors and then buzzed at reception, I had never felt more alone in my life. I'd never imagined my first day at big school to be quite so disorganised. 'I can do this,' I muttered. The receptionist stared at me blankly, before pointing to the left, to a series of offices.

'See the head,' she said. My imagination conjured up an alien head sitting on a desk, maybe with green tentacles reaching out to the phone and the computer, all dripping with acidic slime.

The head turned out to be a massive woman called Mrs Hip, who did have a body after all. I couldn't help but notice her first name was Christine, meaning she was literally 'Chip'. She smelled of vinegar, too, quite like the acidic slime thing, actually, and I couldn't stop myself wrinkling my nose. She stopped her welcoming speech until I looked up and put my listening face on again. When she had warbled about the rules and the fire escapes for ten minutes, she passed me out to a bored secretary in the adjoining room who actually tutted when she pulled up my records and ran her eyes down all of my previous schools. Like it was my fault we kept moving around. *It's not!* I wanted to shout. *You try having a mother who hates staying in one place.* She's not normal, I swear. I had to fill in a million forms and it was hard to remember my new address. 'Darkling Manor' I did recall, but I had no idea about the postcode.

'*Darkling* Manor?' she repeated, looking at me oddly. She leaned in to look through the head's door and waved the papers at her. 'Darkling Manor!' she repeated in an awed tone.

I blinked. What was she on about? Our newest home-for-now did happen to be a particularly odd, creepy house, but I didn't realise they'd know of it.

'Did someone just move out?' I asked.

'A few years ago. It's been empty since then – now what were they...' She tapped her pen on her teeth. 'Ah yes! The Blewitt family. Had a boy here, bit older than you. They barely lasted a month.'

'Sounds like they... blew it?' I cringed at myself but she wasn't listening.

The secretary pulled her cardigan closer and said, 'Everyone around here knows about *that* place.' Her shoulders gave a shudder.

'Oh?' I said politely. 'Really?'

She peered at me over her glasses. 'The tragedy all those years ago! Apparently, the house has never recovered. Nobody has ever really *settled* there. Quite shocking.'

Just as I was bubbling over with questions like a dropped can of pop, she leaned over to the humming copier and handed me a timetable. 'You've missed form time, but if you hurry you won't be late for chemistry with Mr Brand.'

'Oh good,' I said, and she peered sharply at me

in case I was being sarcastic. I kept my face blank.

'Lab four,' she said, handing me a blurry map, pointing at the science labs, which looked to be right over on the other side of the school. Great. I gathered up my backpack and headed out, peeping back at her, hoping for a smile for some stupid reason.

'Get a grip,' I muttered to myself. 'Like I care? I'm not going to be at this school for long either. Mum will finish renovating Darkling and make it all beautiful and shiny again, and then we'll be off to who knows where.' Maybe the far north, I mused, or better still, down south where it was warm and beachy. But most likely it would be somewhere dull and boring again like this place. Castleton, a sprawling village on the edge of a large town. It had sounded smoggy and mucky when we first read about Darkling Manor, but it was actually quite close to lots of green countryside and thick, dark woods. At least it was an improvement on the water mill, I thought. That had been bleak, deep in a valley hemmed in by brown mountains. I still had nightmares about the long icy walk to the outdoor toilet.

My feet followed the map up the scuffed stairs and along a wide grey corridor as my lungs tried to breathe normally. There were a few kids around some lockers, and all of them seemed to sense that I was new, jerking up their heads like lions scenting a gazelle. Maybe panic was sweating out of my pores. At first I tried to smile at everyone who stared at me, but nobody smiled back so I gave up. Down some more stairs, narrow and red this time, and out of a heavy fire door. I checked the map again and looked east, where a huge set of black metal doors had a big sign made out of spanners – *Welcome to Science Block*. I felt a rush of relief. There were a few other kids racing around, obviously late like me. A couple weren't making any attempt to hurry, and I avoided their curious eyes. For the eighth time, I wondered if anyone here would talk to me.

In lab four there was one stool left on a table full of boys, so when the guy I assumed was Mr Brand pointed to it, I shuffled shyly across. I heard whispers and was aware of everyone's eyes on me. I hated and loathed and detested first-day-at-new-school stuff. There were some high-pitched voices so after a while I psyched myself up and was able to glance over toward them. They were mainly coming from the direction of two girls all tucked up together, a brown-haired girl with bright blue eyes and a sharp face, and one who looked like Goldilocks. I kept sneaking glances at them, wishing I had a best friend.

Mr Brand was talking about some atomic

stuff I recognised from the test book Mum had got me, so I took a few minutes to calm down and get my bearings. The boys around me were serious, settling down quickly to the work. One was doing rapid calculations on a massive watch. There was another table of boys behind me and I was very glad I didn't have to sit with them. They were obviously the class idiots and smart-mouths. Mr Brand had to keep shutting them up, until he lost his temper and sent the ringleader away to Mrs Hip. The kid acted all dramatic, throwing his books into his bag and making his mates laugh again. After he'd flounced away, everyone settled down, and when Mr Brand paired us up, I worked with calculator-watch boy, who was called Rob. He seemed decent, but my words were sticking in my throat, so he probably thought I was either stupid or stuck up. It's what everyone always thought.

The lesson finished, and I accelerated from calm-ish to level-ten panic when everyone packed up and split off in a thousand different directions. I was fumbling for my timetable when the blue-eyed girl sauntered over.

'Hello,' she said, eyeing me like a crow eyes a worm. 'Who are you?' She managed to sound cold and disdainful and also like she didn't even care who I was anyway. Her nose was screwed up like something smelled bad.

'I'm B...Bella.' I held my hand up to wave, like some sort of idiot.

Her eyes were startlingly blue, but chilly like the Arctic. Her glossy dark hair made them stand out, but something about her face told me I needed to be on my guard. The one good thing about going to loads of different schools was I had built up an innate sense of who to watch out for. She reminded me of a rainforest snake, beautiful and eye-catching but, underneath it all, a deadly cold-blooded thing.

'Well, *B...Belly*,' she said, 'I'm Skylar.' She glanced to check her friend was flanking her. 'If you need anything, don't ask me!' She burst out laughing, and the other one joined in.

'It's *Bella*... actually,' I whispered. Then I nodded. Funn-ee. 'Got it.'

'I'm joking, of course,' she purred, her arm suddenly threaded in mine. I fought the urge to shake her off. Her skin was cool. She leaned in close and rested her head on my shoulder for a second. I didn't dare breathe, not knowing what to do or say. 'It must be *so* hard to be the new girl. You don't know anything, do you?'

'I'll b...b...be OK,' I mumbled, glancing around to see if anyone else was still nearby.

A scruffy-looking girl caught my attention. She was still packing up her bag, while also tapping on her phone, opening a cereal bar and somewhat nervously glancing towards Skylar. I backed away from the evil pair with a feeble smile and a whispered 'bye then...' and moved towards her.

'Can't she even talk properly?' I heard Skylar ask Goldilocks.

I flushed and remembered my speech therapy

training, taking a deep breath. 'H...Hi?' I said to the scruffy girl, trying to stop shaking. 'I'm Bella.'

She looked up at me, and I prayed that she would be friendly.

'Look,' she said, and I swallowed. 'You watch yourself with that girl, right? I'm just saying.' She gathered up her stuff and swallowed the last of the cereal bar. With that, she walked out. I stared after her, until Mr Brand shooed me out of the lab.

I was surprised to see she was waiting for me a little further on.

'I'm Lex.' She had short shaggy hair that was a gingery red and funky purple-framed glasses. 'Where have you come from anyway?'

'I j...just moved here. I change schools a lot because of my mum's job,' I said. I was relieved that my voice worked in front of Lex. *Keep taking deep breaths, and the words will flow*, I told myself. I knew I was still blushing, because my face burned and talking to new people was hard. Sometimes if I was really nervous, I stuttered, or worst-case scenario, my words got stuck and I couldn't speak at all.

'We were in Wales for ages, but now we're in a place called Darkling Manor here—'

'Wait.' She held up a hand, palm facing me. 'Darkling?!' she gasped. '*Manor...*?!' Her eyes spread open behind her glasses. 'You actually *live* there? Are you serious?'

'Yes,' I replied slowly, thinking about the secretary's reaction to the place and now Lex's. I narrowed my eyes. 'What's wrong with it?'

'Oh, nothing. Nothing at all. It's just a massive black-bricked mansion with its own clock tower that isn't weird and threatening and unusual at all,' said Lex, shaking her head like mad. 'It definitely wouldn't be *completely* terrifying to actually *live* there...'

She simultaneously nodded at my timetable and pulled out her phone. 'We have history next,' she said. A crumb from the cereal bar fell off her chin. Then accelerated and I had to jog to keep up. We zoomed down the science block stairs, and I tried to concentrate on which way she was leading me.

'Sit by me and I'll tell you all about your new home.'

I nodded, a tiny warm glow in my chest as I realised I had actually found someone to talk to.

'But you must already know?' she said.

'Know? About what?' I asked as we bumped through the big metal science doors.

'Oh, that Darkling is famous around Castleton for one main reason.'

'What's that?' I said, diving out of the way of some tall kids chasing a football. Hadn't the secretary chattered about a tragedy? Lex bowled straight through other kids, whereas I ducked and dodged around them until I was out of breath.

She faced me, shaking her head. 'I can't believe you haven't sensed anything. I'm *sure* I would have. I'm something of an expert, after all.' She noticed my puzzled expression and grabbed my arm. 'You don't know, do you?

There are stories about the place that would scare you stupid!'

I stared at her, frowning. But inside I did know. My brain was working at warp speed as I considered the front door that misbehaved. The piano scales. And, most of all, the cold whispering in my ear.

'There's a little chapel in the back garden!' Her eyes widened and she leaned closer. 'I did a research project on it a few years ago, just for fun. In like 1888, a vicar *died* in there! A newspaper said he was broken-hearted after losing his only daughter...'

'Alexandrina?' came a sharp voice. 'How about less talking and more walking to your lesson!'

We sped away from the fierce teacher, who was clutching a coffee cup and policing the corridors.

'What?' I said, trying to catch my breath and Lex's eye. A vicar? A daughter? 'Did she... play the piano?'

But Lex was busy squabbling with a huge boy who had elbowed her in the head and we were already lining up outside a sunny classroom.

A small woman in a tight army jacket marched towards us like a soldier and I was surprised when the class instantly fell silent.

'Right,' she snapped. 'File in.'

I followed Lex over to the back and pulled out the chair next to hers.

'We have a new student,' said the teacher, peering over huge square-shaped glasses. 'Where are you, Bella Bright?'

I raised my hand and she nodded. 'I don't know what history you've done but we're studying the canals and waterways of Great Britain.' I tried to smile and nod as she handed out worksheets. 'I'm Miss Wilton and I will assess you soon enough.'

'Major Wilton,' whispered Lex. 'She was in the army before teaching. As you can probably tell.'

I could see that Major Wilton wouldn't tolerate messing about, so I settled down to work, feeling oddly happy, which was super unusual for day one in a new school.

I snuck looks at Lex from under my fringe and heard her humming to herself as she smudged and scrawled the answers on her sheet.

Skylar and Goldilocks weren't in this lesson, and lots of different kids who hadn't been in chemistry were. Rob with his calculator watch raised a hand to wave at me and I smiled back. Maybe, just *maybe* this school would be OK. Was it possible the kids could even be nice? I thought of all the worrying I'd done. There was still time for everything to go wrong.

'You have reading in the library next,' whispered Lex after a quick glance at my timetable. The bell rang and everyone started packing up. 'I'll see you at lunch, OK?'

I nodded and checked my map for the library. I was already tired, with a million new impressions rattling around my brain. New names, faces, directions. I thought of Mum and wished that for once she had a normal job where we could stay in the same place for more than a few months at a time. Something in human resources or a bank, maybe. I tried to imagine her, all messy black hair with pencils sticking out of it, tape measures around her neck, site boots. She'd wilt in an office, like an exotic flower in the wrong soil. I peeked at the toes of my own steel-capped site boots, half-wishing for some normal school shoes like the other girls. I didn't have spares, as all the packing and unpacking meant that we both travelled extremely lightly.

It was a shame that as soon as houses and manors looked gorgeous and had things like bright gleaming swimming pools and marshmallow leather settees, we quickly moved on to the next ramshackle project. The nastiest ones had infestations of rats and mice, and even cockroaches. I complained that it was worse than living in prison, but Mum just laughed.

'It's character-building,' she'd always say, usually chucking me under the chin. 'Makes you appreciate the good stuff, doesn't it, Bells my darling?'

The library was easy to find, but my heart sank like a stone when I saw the deadly duo were there too. 'Awesome,' I sighed inwardly and tried to subtly drift to the far side of the room to avoid them, but they wolf-packed around me.

'Hello, Bella!' said Skylar, and I tried to paste on a smile. Her sharp little chin reminded me of an evil pixie.

'Here's the thing,' she went on, screwing up her face. 'There's a mad rumour that you live in Darkling Manor... and...'

'I d...do,' I whispered.

'Oh!' Skylar peered amazedly at Goldilocks. 'It is true! Our shy little noob must be rich!'

'I'm n...not rich,' I said quickly. 'We don't own the place. We're living in it while my m...mum does it up. She's a designer...'

'Oh!' Skylar nodded, her eyes gleaming. 'So you're *literally* squatting.'

'N...no!' I said.

She looked thrilled to have got a rise out of me, so I bit my lip, staring at the floor. My heart was thumping and I felt dizzy.

'Squatting is such a filthy word, isn't it?' She looked at her friend for support. Goldilocks nodded rapidly.

'Gosh,' Skylar went on. 'I don't understand it at all. You live in it, but don't own it. I didn't know you could *steal* a house! I suppose it doesn't matter anyway. Nobody else has lived there for years, after all! By the way, a little advice to a noob.' She looked around and leaned in closer. 'You could be a bit friendlier, you know.'

Wait. '*Steal* a house?' I tried not to splutter. 'We d...didn't steal it! The owner is p...paying my mum...' I bit my lip, frustrated that my stutter was getting worse around these girls. I tried to take some deep breaths. Mum's face floated into my mind and nodded encouragingly.

They looked sceptical and I peeped at them in turn. I breathed again and tried to keep my voice level. 'Anyway. I am friendly?' I finished weakly.

'Oh good! Because it's Halloween on Friday, and we would love one thing more than anything.' Skylar pressed in tighter to me until I could see her eyeliner flicks. 'One thing that only you, Bella, could make happen.' Her heavy perfume tickled my nose. 'You just *have* to invite us for a spooky sleepover!'

'Oh...' I gulped. 'I don't know... I'm sorry.' I tried to think rapidly. 'My mum's out at a conference that night, and I'm supposed to just stay in and do my schoolwork...'

'Your mum's away? Leaving you all alone at Darkling Manor for *Halloween*?' Goldilocks was shaking her head. 'That's got to be child abandonment! Totally illegal.'

'That's Regan,' said Skylar, pointing at her. 'Regan Effiyong, to be precise. Her dad is a barrister and she knows an awful lot about the law. So listen to her, OK?'

Regan pulled at a ringlet of her hair and inclined her chin at me like she was royal or something. Her almond-shaped eyes were dark brown and warmer than Skylar's. I blinked from one to the other.

'We won't take no for an answer!' Skylar started whooping. 'Sleepover party!'

'Who's having a party?' Rob leaned back on a

chair to edge into our conversation, and I gave him a double-take in shock. There was no way I could have a party or a sleepover at the property, no way at all. And definitely not with boys. I mean, I'd never really had any friends, but certainly never ever any *boy*friends. I tried to imagine Mum's face if she found out there would be a boy sleeping over. Wait! What about the house? What if it got damaged? *But hold on... it already is damaged*, I reminded myself. Mum hadn't actually done much of anything yet, and admittedly the thought of being alone there all Halloween evening until she got back was sort of creepy, actually. Should I answer the door to trick or treaters, or ignore them? It was gruesome enough in bright sunshine at midday, let alone in the gloomy dark on Halloween. Maybe having some company of my own wouldn't hurt... and maybe it would help me make some real friends. I looked at Skylar high-fiving Regan. Maybe they were my friends now? Did this count? Was this what friends did? I wasn't sure.

Somehow it didn't really feel exactly... friendly?

'Yes, Bella!' said Skylar gleefully. 'Are you coming, Rob? For Halloween at Darkling?'

'Darkling?!' He stared at me with big eyes. 'Are you serious?'

I pulled a face. 'I'm awfully s...sorry, but I won't be allowed boys.'

Skylar rolled her eyes. 'Good grief, Belly, your squatting mother is strict. But she won't *be* there, remember?'

'Nobody else. I'm serious, OK?' I let my worry funnel down into some vocal force and narrowed my eyes at Skylar. She nodded, holding up her hands in mock defeat.

'Fine. Have it your way. Just us girls. A private sleepover.'

The librarian hurried over and shushed us, and I looked down at the floor, my heart thumping. What had I done?

5

The bell rang for lunchtime at last and I followed the mass stampede into the dining room, looking out for Lex. There was no sign of her, so in the end I sat on an empty table and pulled out my initial photos and quick sketches of Darkling. I munched on a tuna sandwich I'd made earlier, when there was a sudden clattering of feet and screech of chairs and then the deadly duo were around me again. I tried to look happy about it. What was wrong with me that only these two were interested in me? Was it better to have no friends at all than bad friends? I felt guilty for judging. I'd only known them a couple of hours. More likely it was me who was a bad friend.

My head raced around in circles as I swallowed and tried to smile at them.

'What you got there?' asked Regan, twirling her hair again.

'M...my lunch?' I waved the sandwich. She shook her head.

'No, silly. Those!' She pointed at the pile of pictures.

'I h...help my mum out by taking the photographs she needs, for referencing wood and...'

'Yawnsville,' said Skylar, rolling her eyes. 'Are you serious? Child labour? I certainly hope your mummy pays you a decent wage.' She elbowed Regan. 'Maybe you had better tell your dad about poor Bella.' She looked at me again. 'Regan's dad could represent you in court, and you could divorce her.'

I stiffened at the word 'divorce'. I'd had enough of all that for a lifetime. She blathered on, talking about Regan's dad's white wig, and how legal action would only cost 'a couple of thou, max'.

I looked down at my lunch. She was a bad friend. It was none of her business how I got on with my mum. We did lots of work together, and I loved it. I collated the photography for the files and updated the Bright Interiors website but also got involved with the actual cleaning and decorating. I was always free to research gargoyles and help her choose between their ugly little faces. Often Mum would need to do something really detailed and painstaking, and I always pitched in. Together we fitted the most awkwardly tiny hexagonal tiles, hand-sanded elaborate balustrades, even designed new gargoyle faces. Every job was different and challenging in a new way, and she couldn't do it without me, she always told me. We were a team, after all, and the important thing was, since the divorce I didn't want to think about, we only really had each other.

'So, this is the famous Darkling Manor, hmm?' asked Regan. She leaned across my pictures, and I forced myself to swallow the bit of tuna sandwich I'd been endlessly chewing since they arrived. I coughed and took a gulp from my bottle of water.

'They're quite good, actually.' She stuck out her bottom lip. 'I always wondered what it looked like inside.'

'Thanks.' While we'd been unpacking the car last night, I had actually been trying to record the weird piano music with my phone. All had stayed quiet, though, and I was starting to think I had imagined it. I'd tried to search playing scales, but the Wi-Fi was off and I had no data. Internet! I remembered. I had to get Mum to sort it.

Skylar rolled her eyes again. 'I hope you have some cool games for your sleepover,' she said. 'We wouldn't want it to be *boring*, now, would we?'

I guessed she didn't exactly mean Snap or Boggle. Then I thought about the whisper again. *'Play my game.'* Everyone here wanted to play games, it seemed.

Regan seemed unsure whether to nod or

shake her head at the 'boring' comment, and ended up turning it in circles, saying, 'I could bring my manicure sets?'

'Oh, not nails *again*!' Skylar mocked her. 'I'm bored of nails. It's Halloween, remember? We need spooky entertainment. *I'll* have a think.'

Regan started chewing her own nails.

'And I want us to have cool Gothic bedrooms.' Skylar was still talking, like a demanding toddler. For a second I wondered how Regan put up with her, before I remembered the real bedrooms at Darkling. I'd only had a chance to look in a few of them, but the problems were all similar. The wallpaper hanging off the rotting walls, everything growing over with mould and the dust-covered cobwebs in the eaves. Oh well. She said she wanted spooky...

'Regan?' barked Skylar, when she saw her still flipping through the pictures. 'We have dance class now.'

'Sure,' said Regan after a moment, sniffing.

'See you later,' said Skylar, managing to make it sound unpleasant.

My forehead hit the table after they'd left the room.

'What's up?' asked an alarmed voice, and I jerked up to see Lex looking down at me.

'Those girls,' I said. 'Skylar and Regan.'

'Oh man.' Lex shook her head. 'The deadly duo. I warned you about them.'

'I tried to be careful,' I said.

She nodded. 'You have to be on your guard when you're speaking to people like that. They'll take advantage of you.' She sniffed. 'They used to be like that with me...' She pulled her glasses off and cleaned them.

'Sorry to hear that,' I said, screwing up my face. 'I'm in trouble already, I think. They've somehow sort of invited themselves over on Halloween for a sleepover party.' I fiddled with my sandwich wrapper. 'I don't know how to get out of it.'

'Oh, well, that's mega-bad news for you.

They'll never give up. You may as well just roll over and let Skylar do whatever she wants.' She unpacked her own lunch and popped a can of lemonade. I watched her, feeling miserable.

She looked stern for a moment, fussing about with her sandwich before looking at me again.

'I suppose I'll have to step in.' She narrowed her eyes. 'You need protecting from them.' She popped and slurped from her can. 'I'll have to come too.'

I blinked. 'What?'

She stared back and swallowed. 'But... only if you want me to...?' She flushed bright red until her cheeks matched her hair. I felt a huge grin bend my mouth.

'*Want* you to? Are you s...serious? Of course I would!' I beamed. 'But obviously only if *you* really want to?' As I asked the question, I blushed too. If she changed her mind and said no now, I thought I might die. Did she even like me at all, or was she simply keeping track of the deadly duo? I chewed my lip. Why was making friends so complicated?

'Actually, I can't wait to see the place,' she said. 'The pics you have here are crazy.'

I grinned at her in relief. I wondered what she'd think about the whispering! But something told me to keep that secret for now. I didn't want to seem *too* weird, after all. I was already the new girl, not very good at talking, annoyingly shy.

We looked at the images, pointing at the dark wood interior, the rotting floorboards, broken, dusty furniture and cracked checkerboard tiles. I recalled how everything was seemingly held together by more cobwebs than a ghost train. It would be nuts on Halloween; Skylar was right about that. Then the bell rang and everyone started getting up.

'It's afternoon registration,' said Lex. 'You're in same form as me, room 21, English block. Let's go.'

It was so nice to have someone to follow around, I mused. I had gotten lost several times at the last school, Carston Primary, which had been massive. Once, the caretaker there had mistakenly shut me in a supply cupboard. He had eventually freed me, horrified by his mistake, but I was more upset that nobody had actually missed me.

My new form tutor, Miss Jones, made me stand up and introduce myself. There is nothing more awkward in the entire world. I peeked around at my new form, half of them asleep, the other half watching keenly in case I fell over or vomited down my blazer. Deeply glad that Skylar wasn't there, I managed to stammer a few bits, but luckily a boy farted and everyone turned away from me and roared with laughter. Miss Jones rolled her eyes and moved smartly on to notices and announcements. I sat down in a hurry, wanting to thank him, despite the awful smell.

Walking home from school with Lex turned out to be way more fun than walking alone. As we got further away from the red gates, she described all of the teachers and kids in our classes in enormous detail. Who had the best eyebrows – a Year 11 girl called Hannah Kaur – and poor Arthur Macbride, who had fallen over on the first day, tearing his trousers and showing his questionable pants to the entire school.

There was a huge row of golden trees to our left, and they swished in the cool wind like cheerleader pompoms. Leaves were falling, and I was glad. Summer had dragged on long enough. I felt pretty good about school for once, but when Lex asked

44

if I preferred Springhill to my other schools, I remembered with a pang that I probably wouldn't be here for long. Lex looked sideways at me and I tried to smile.

'Thanks for today,' I said. 'You didn't have to help me out, I know. You've been great. Really.'

'Well, thanks too. I feel like you need my help with the deadly duo. Believe me... I *get* Skylar. But also because you may not have noticed but I'm not exactly drowning in friends, you know.'

She said it lightly but I heard inside her words. She was staring at her feet.

'We actually make our own duo. We could be the... dangerous duo?' I smiled.

'And maths can be our secret weapon. Two duos make a very odd quad!' She giggled as we crossed over a small road.

'We definitely have all the right angles.'

'Better a quad than a circle. Circles are so pointless...'

I laughed, the fresh wind blowing in my face.

Lex elbowed me. 'Do you know what my favourite kind of tree is?'

I shrugged. 'An oak?'

'No... geometry.' We cracked up laughing, finally out of puns.

'Look,' I blurted suddenly. 'Do you want to come around to Darkling to see the place from the inside? We could have some crisps and an apple?' I had surprised myself and hung there breathless as I waited for her answer.

'OK,' she said. 'Cool.'

'Great.' I grinned at her, relief whooshing through my blood, marvelling at how easy that had been.

'So tired,' muttered Lex, blowing hair off her face. 'Why is it uphill all the way to yours?'

I had to laugh. 'It's not!'

A couple more twists and turns, and it was in front of us. We stood and looked at Darkling squatting on the side of the road, set far back from all the other houses. There was a preservation order on it because it was so old, and something to do with the tiny chapel ruins at the back. Around it, the other houses looked shiny and new. Darkling stood out like a monster's thumb on a human hand.

The sun was behind it now, like when I'd first seen the place. It shimmered behind the dark brick. The roof tiles seemed to bulge and shrink, like they were the huge scales of some enormous reptile. Maybe a dragon, I thought. Lex halted on the pavement and shaded her eyes with her hands.

'Woah,' she said. 'You live in the most crazy, scary house in the whole world.'

I tried to put myself in her place, examining the details for the first time. Three floors topped with the strange clock tower. The small, dirty windows, with the ivy clambering up the front like it was trying to strangle the place. The chimney pots were wonky and several roof tiles had already given up the fight against gravity. The shards crunched underfoot as we stepped closer.

Beside us ran the long, thin front lawns, tangled with spiky bushes and choking with weeds.

'Welcome,' I said in a fake-cheerful tone. 'Before us, I believe the Addams family lived here.'

'The who? It's the kind of place that needs a family of vampires,' Lex said.

I rolled my eyes. 'That's who the Addams family basically were! Mum wanted to call me Wednesday...'

'Woah! Was that the day you were born?'

'Erm... no. She's a character? With long dark plaits like mine?'

She wasn't listening, though, but staring upwards. She pointed to the tower. 'Your clock has stopped.'

'Even a stopped clock tells the right time twice a day.' I quoted the old saying as I pulled out my massive key and joggled it in the ancient lock. With a creak, the bolt clanked and the door pulled its usual trick of falling open violently, hanging at an odd angle on its huge hinges.

'Is there anybody there...?' called Lex as she leaned in, and her voice echoed in the hallway.

'Mum's out,' I said. 'It'll just be us.'

'Great,' said Lex doubtfully. We stared at each other before I clambered up the wonky step and entered the house. All around me it seemed hushed, like the house was holding its breath. Lex followed me closely, and then jumped as the door slammed.

I swallowed.

'I didn't touch it!' Lex exclaimed.

I placed the key on the floor by the hideous vase again, flashing her a smile. Maybe she thought the wind had blown it closed or something. Then I remembered it opened inwards. A faulty hinge, then? I braced myself for her questions but Lex was quiet, staring around, an awestruck expression on her face. I double-checked the key was safe as Mum had told me to be careful with it until she could cut another spare. I wondered if it would even be possible, or if she'd have to ask the devil to forge a second one in the fires of hell. I shook my head, watching Lex. 'Try and be normal,' I murmured to myself.

'What did you say?' She looked at me.

'Nothing.' I bit the inside of my cheek.

'These tiles are making me dizzy!' said Lex, staring down.

'I don't look directly at them,' I said, covering my eyes with my hands. 'They're a health hazard.'

We dropped our backpacks in the hallway on the cleanest section of the floor and walked along to the end that was the door for the kitchen.

'Ugh,' said Lex at the slimy green cabinets. Many years ago there must have been a leak that nobody had cleared up, leaving mildew and rot everywhere. We'd scrubbed out about half of the cupboards and stowed our supplies. I grabbed some crisps and pointed to the fruit bowl for Lex to choose from the red apples. We wandered into the back lounge, sitting on the sofa Mum had got from the charity shop. She'd been busy while I'd been at school. It was clean, and actually very comfortable. I wished it was *really* our sofa, instead of a temporary fix for a strange house that belonged to a strange woman who lived miles away.

'The owner is called Mrs Hallorann,' I said. 'She looks like an ostrich.'

'She sounds... unusual,' said Lex, crunching away on her apple.

'Yeah,' I said. I'd noticed the cobwebs festooning the ceiling and I hoped Lex wasn't freaked out by spiders. This place had more spiders than Brazil. I shuddered. No walking around in bare feet.

It was then that we heard the footsteps.

*Thunk, thunk, **thunk***. Right over our heads. I swallowed the piece of apple I'd been chewing and glanced at Lex. She'd heard them too and was frowning up at the cracked ceiling.

'Erm, who's that?' she asked. Her face seemed to wriggle through a thousand expressions.

I opened my mouth but no sound came out. There was nobody else here.

'Shall we go and see?' She stood up, and I followed her, a shard of ice tingling down my spine.

'Do we have to?' I asked, as we walked back out of the lounge and into the hallway. 'I mean... we could just go out for a bit till Mum gets home...' My voice was a bit shrieky, but Lex ignored me.

The main stairs faced the front door and curved up steeply, but she bounded up them like a mountain goat. 'Wait!' I whispered, wanting to listen again, but she'd already turned around the curve. I followed, moving faster, my breath catching as I realised she'd gone up out of sight. In certain places the floors weren't safe, and Bob the surveyor still hadn't been. I prayed she wouldn't run over a rotten section and go crashing through to the room below.

'Lex?' I called in a low voice as I made it onto the landing. I peered left and right, and then heard a sharp scream. 'Lex!' I shouted. 'Lex!?' I ran to the left where the scream seemed to come from and stared wildly into the doorways I passed.

At last I found her, hand on her throat, facing a puzzled man holding a piece of pipe and a wrench.

'Sorry, ladies,' he said. 'Mrs Bright left me here to finish the shower.'

'**WOAH**,' Lex was saying, and I forced a smile at the man.

'Sorry about that,' I said, grabbing Lex's shoulders and marching her back to the stairs. 'Are you OK?'

'I thought you said there was nobody else here!'

'I forgot! Mum probably figured we needed hot water and a working shower. Actually, I think she did tell me this morning but I was so flustered about school...'

Lex was shaking, and I drew back, ready to apologise again. 'Look, I'm sorry, alright, the house is creepy and I should've remembered he'd be here... but...'

Then I realised she was shaking with laughter.
'Oh my goodness, Bella. I thought he was a ghost!
Can you believe it! A *ghost*!'

I tried my best to laugh along.

7

Over Wednesday and Thursday, I worked hard after school on the first two bedrooms to the left of the staircase, hoping to make them a little more presentable for the sleepover. One was the pink room I had bravely adopted as my own after hoovering the ceiling, and the other had clearly once been blue. Now it was largely grey and beige with mould, although a cluster of orange wall-toadstools certainly brightened it somewhat. Mum strode past with some wallpaper samples and skidded to a halt, admiring what I was doing. I took a deep breath.

'There are some kids at school, Mum, who want to come to a little... sleepover here tomorrow night, for Halloween?'

She twisted her mouth to the side and narrowed one eye.

'There's a really nice girl called Lex, and she's sort of my best friend.' I crossed my fingers behind my back. 'And you'll be away...' I played the guilt card with wide, innocent eyes.

'I'll be home by midnight,' Mum said, folding her arms. 'And what will you all be doing here? The floors aren't particularly safe yet, you know. Bob's here tomorrow morning at least, but you'll need to be really careful.'

'Yes, so that's why I'm sorting the bedrooms on our side.' I pointed. 'I'll make sure everyone stays clear of the right-hand side.' The right-hand side looked bumpy and odd, so we'd stayed off it. Plus it was the way to the attics and the clock tower, so it was best to just avoid. I felt hope creep through my chest as I realised she was sort of agreeing.

'And *nobody* goes in the clock tower.' She sounded fierce. 'Even I haven't checked up there yet.

Mrs Hallorann never tried it. Bob's already looked at the plans and said he's too big to get up there to inspect it thoroughly, so we may decide to seal it or take it down. And leave the second floor alone. And the attics. Promise me?'

I nodded, trying not to grin in delight.

'Right. I'll get you some food and snacks in, and you'd better behave yourselves.'

'I always behave!' I protested, and she surprised me by grabbing me in a huge hug. I held on tightly, not wanting to be the first to let go.

'I know you do. And I'm very glad you're settling in, Bells,' she said in my ear. I squirmed out of her arms but I was smiling. This could be good! I couldn't wait to text Lex. I'd have to walk to the road to do it, though.

On Friday morning, my alarm didn't go off, and I was horribly late.

'You'll have to run,' said Mum, calmly eating toast and slurping coffee. 'My train leaves soon.'

I scowled at her but she reached up to tug gently on my plait.

'I'll miss you, Bells. Remember I'll be gone when you get back, so don't forget your key, OK?'

'Have a good conference, Mum.'

'I love you, my little girl.' She half stood to kiss my cheek and I smiled.

'I'm taller than you already, Mum.'

'You won't even need a ladder soon!' Her eyes were sparkling. 'You'll have to bend down to clean the guttering!'

'OK, ha ha. Also, the guttering is your job.'

We always missed each other when she went to conferences. Everything always seemed so quiet when she was away. I kissed her head, grabbing her last piece of toast and managing to escape the front door without it booting me out. I frowned back at Darkling as I walked down the drive and went flying over a lump of brick lying on the ground. Stupid house. For a second I thought I saw something in one of the upstairs windows, but then I blinked and there was nothing.

'Halloween spookiness,' I told myself as I chomped the last mouthful of toast, shivering. It had gone cold, and the trees were shaking down their leaves. Autumn was truly here, and I wriggled my toes in my boots. The best time of year. The little shops near us in Castleton were full of plastic orange pumpkin heads and white fake cobwebs, purple witch wigs and sweets to hand to trick-or-treaters. Mum had offered to buy some for the party but I'd raised my arms to the house and laughed at her. We had so many miles of the real thing there was no need to buy any fakery. She bought two massive pumpkins instead, and we'd carved them on the big pine kitchen table, another charity shop treasure. Mine was leering and scary, whereas hers had a big cute grin. She'd put them on the wonky step outside the house, and we'd laughed as mine had rolled down the angle to head-butt into hers.

The memory gave me a warm glow. She always made Halloween fun. And Christmas, and Easter, with her famous egg hunt. She was right: I did have to appreciate the good stuff.

At form time, I was thrilled with myself at managing to slip in unnoticed. I found Lex fizzing with excitement. 'I thought you weren't coming in! Imagine if you'd been poorly today of all days! I can't believe it's tonight! Mum's got me some new pyjamas!'

'Great.' I smiled, imagining the grubby, freezing-cold rooms. 'Maybe an old tracksuit would be better?'

'What?' She cocked her head on one side. Then I watched as she caught on. 'Not done much cleaning yet, eh?'

'And not much in the way of central heating either.' I shook my head.

Mum had been all focused on finding the correct shade of periwinkle blue for the kitchen and prepping for the property conference.

We hadn't got much done at all, apart from the pumpkins. She'd been researching her speech, which was all about gargoyles. Darkling didn't even have gargoyles, although she usually added a tiny one somewhere on every restoration, as her calling card.

Later in science, Regan caught my eye. She had dangly earrings on, and they flashed in the lab lights. I had the seat next to Lex and squinted in the sequin glare. Mr Brand was writing on the whiteboard about radiation, and Skylar was in deep conversation with another girl who seemed to be called Flick, who was demonstrating a complex hair braid, and I started watching her for tips. Then Regan slipped me a note.

My eyebrows nearly joined my hairline as I hid it under my palm and acted cool, just as Skylar looked away from Flick's hair and pointed her cold blue gaze straight at me. Lex broke the tense moment by elbowing me too hard in the ribs to ask about number five, and I couldn't help a little groan escape.

'Who's making silly noises?' snapped Mr Brand, whirling around like a bearded ballerina.

Our table assumed innocent faces, big eyes, chins stretched downwards and he scowled at us all in turn before spinning back to face the board.

I dared to check Skylar again, and saw her eyeing Regan, who was writing neatly with her sparkly pen, her earrings still twinkling in the light. I hadn't dared to move my hand, and I started to worry that the sweat would make her message melt.

Steadily, I swooped it under my textbook and then even more slowly down between Lex and me, out of Skylar's view. Mr Brand went over to the noisy boys' table, and I opened it, reading it under cover of the table and Lex's arm.

'What are you looking at?' she whispered, but I shushed her. I was desperate to see what Regan had written, because in the days since Skylar had invited the deadly duo round for the sleepover, they'd both pretty much avoided me.

In beautiful purple writing, it said:

> *Skylar is planning something 4 tonight*

I blinked. Skylar was planning something? Like what? A trick? A performance? A *murder*?

I nudged Lex and she slyly took the note from me. I looked back at Regan, but she was intent on her work.

Was this a real warning? Or a double bluff to make me nervous? Because it certainly did.

'What do you think?' I hissed to Lex, but Mr Brand was bearing down on our table.

'There's a lot of whispering!' he was saying, so we quickly shut up. I didn't get a chance to talk to Lex until we were on our way down from the art room after last bell.

'What do you make of the note?' I asked.

'*Note* a lot,' she quipped, her eyes shining

behind her glasses. 'It's a *write* mystery.'

'Seriously, Lex!'

'The duo are a tricky pair,' she said. 'They might be doing a spooky Halloween-type thing, you know, dressing up as vampires, or something.' She leaned towards me. '*Or* they might not be doing anything, and Regan is just winding you up for her own amusement.'

I nodded, chewing my finger. Anything was possible, I guessed. I'd only known these girls a couple of days.

She tapped her chin. 'Or... Regan is *pretending* Skylar doesn't know she's warning you but it's all an act and *Skylar* is actually the one behind it all.'

'Behind what?' I asked, feeling more confused.

'Behind something to make you look silly.' Lex nodded firmly.

'Yeah,' I said slowly. I watched my feet on the stairs as everyone thundered down around us. 'But what if it's something worse?' I whispered.

65

'Worse?' she repeated as we made it through the doors into the chilly air. 'Is there *anything* worse than being made fun of by Skylar and Regan?'

I pulled my coat around me and stuck my hands deep in the pockets. Lex sounded so sour, I wondered what they had done to her.

'Before you came here... they were mean to me.' She swallowed. 'They called me some awful things, you know, and once I'm sure Skylar tripped me up in PE. I went flying and broke my glasses. Everyone laughed.' She looked miserable.

'Well,' I said, 'I'm here now. They'll be mean to me instead.' I tried to smile.

'I'm glad I've got you,' she said, and I smiled for real.

'So you think they're really planning something mean?'

'They literally have no kindness in them.' Lex shook her head.

'Yeah! But... what if they're going to sabotage my house or something? Like break stuff?' I tried to get my feeling of dread into words. This whole sleepover was a terrible idea, an awful plan. Why hadn't I been quicker to say no?

Lex bumped into me gently as we walked, and I looked up at her.

'Whatever it is, Bella, I'll be there. We can handle anything those two try. We will defeat them.'

I raised an eyebrow. 'You planning on stealing their shoes?'

She chuckled. '*De-feet*. I like it.' And gave me a fist-bump.

Her confidence inspired me, and after a moment I took a deep breath and grinned.

By half past six that evening, I was not smiling. Everyone was coming over at seven and nothing was ready. I'd had a shower and got most of my homework finished as I hated it hanging on through the weekend. Mum had been shopping for me and there were things like popcorn and crisps, marshmallows and lemonade. There still weren't any decorations aside from the two pumpkins at the front, and now I pictured Skylar's unimpressed face and wished I'd gone a bit more to town. This was my first party, after all. Like... ever. Then I stared at the house and told myself firmly that it really didn't need any decorations. It was already as creepy as a graveyard at midnight. Maybe I could get the whisperer to terrify everyone, though I ruled the thought out almost as soon as I had it. It would be better if nothing strange happened, to be honest. I had enough to deal with just having them here.

Around me there were creaks and clicks as the ancient heating came on, the chilly radiators bubbling and groaning. I supposed I should be grateful for it, even though it seemed to make the house colder rather than warmer.

The ceilings above me were high and the rooms empty aside from our charity shop bits, the remains of old broken furniture and thick layers of dust like dirty icing sugar. Outside it was cold and dark, the wind whipping the trees around, making the branches tap at the windows like knobbly skeleton fingers.

Maybe they'd all cancel if the weather turned bad, I thought. A nice quiet night in would be so much better than this nervous spinning of my stomach. I wondered again about Regan's note, and what, if anything, Skylar had planned. But why had Regan warned me? Was it all lies designed to make me worry? I worried about being too worried, and then worried some more about maybe not worrying enough. Just as I'd tied myself into some impressive mental knots, the house fell deathly silent as though it was waiting for something to happen. I held my breath too, staring at the lounge walls, where immense pictures had hung and the colours of the peeling wallpaper were lighter.

The door knocker banged.

I hoped it would be Lex, but of course it was the duo. When I pulled open the door, they walked in together, clutching one another, crab-like, and Skylar pulled out her mobile phone, which was massive and shiny gold.

'I can't believe we're actually in here!' she declared. 'Spooky selfie!'

Regan nodded at Skylar, her eyes zipping everywhere. I tried to see what they saw, the splintered dark-wood staircase, the half-polished checkerboard floor, the massive red glass vase shaped like a screaming woman, which stood in an alcove beside us and had my broken umbrella popping out of the top.

'I need to text my parents that I'm here safely,' went on Skylar. I watched them both like they were slightly dangerous animals, unsure how to behave now they were actually, really here at Darkling.

'Wait!' hissed Skylar.

I blinked in surprise.

'My phone won't work!'

Regan pulled her pink smartphone out and started typing frantically. 'Nor mine!' she said, and for a long moment I thought she was about to cry.

'Oh, g...guys,' I said, and they peered at me for the first time. 'Phones don't work very well here.'

'Phones don't *what*?' shrieked Skylar, starting to hyperventilate. 'I need my phone beside me at all times! My mum says I have to be in touch all day and all night!'

Regan looked mournfully at hers and switched it off. 'I can deal.' She shrugged. 'It's only one night.'

'Yes! One WHOLE night!' Skylar wouldn't be comforted. Then she looked at me and pursed up her lips. 'You could have warned us. Why don't phones work here?' she asked.

I shrugged. 'Something about the walls? It can't receive the aerial? I've no idea, really.' I tried to look unconcerned, but I was worried that these two would be a massive headache about their phones. 'The Wi-Fi is so p...patchy it drives Mum mad when she's trying to work. O...on our second day it took four hours to send one email.' I tried to close my own mouth with my hand, aware that I was both stammering and rambling. I was relieved to see that they weren't listening anyway, pointing out the overpowering dark wood ceiling and whispering to each other.

Actually, I was thrilled that phones wouldn't work, as I knew neither of them could instantly post anything they filmed or photographed all over the internet. And I just knew they would be out to cause me max embarrassment. Hah. I felt a mix of guilt and relief as I watched them slowly put their precious phones away. I narrowed my eyes. Was Skylar's plan now ruined because of the lack of internet?

Then the knocker banged again and we all jumped. I moved to yank it open, but Skylar got there first.

'Yes,' she said imperiously. I folded my arms and tried not to roll my eyes at her cheek.

It was Lex, her red hair soggy. It had started to rain. Behind her, Darkling's driveway looked bleak and gloomy, curving down to the street lights that twinkled in the dark and seemed a long way away.

'Come in costume, have you, Alexandrina?' said Skylar mockingly. 'Or maybe not, because you always look scary.'

'Hi, Lex!' I said, ignoring Skylar. The others moved away from the door, blanking us both.

I took Lex's bag and left it near the bottom of the stairs, and we grinned at each other.

'Bet you're glad to see me!' said Lex, nudging me with her elbow as the duo wandered off.

'Yes!' I said. 'Those two are—'

I was interrupted by shrieks from the lounge. Lex and I looked at each other, before I bounced through to see what was upsetting the duo so much. I was half-worried they might have heard the whisper, so I tried to think of some old house explanations. Condensation... magnetism... the wind in the chimneys.

'It's filthy!' said Skylar, rubbing her fingers together like she was Mary Poppins inspecting the nursery.

I cast a critical eye around the room and shrugged. She was lucky she hadn't seen it on day one! I'd have hoovered again if the vacuum cleaner hadn't blown up, and Mum hadn't washed her eco-cloths yet with all the flurry of packing for her gargoyle conference. Surreptitiously,

I pushed some random laundry underneath the charity shop sofa with my foot and tried to look innocent.

'What on earth is growing in the carpet?' said Skylar, peering down at something on the floor.

'There are some snacks in the kitchen,' I said to divert everyone. The array of fungus in this house was truly astonishing.

'Urgh, who knows what we'll find in there! Am I right, Regan?' Skylar held up a hand for her to high five, but Regan was watching something in the corner.

'What's that down there?' she said, squinting.

I followed her gaze and then winced as Skylar let out a piercing scream.

'A mouse!' said Lex, rushing forward and kneeling down to get a closer look. 'What a sweet little thing!' It scurried back down a gap in the skirting board and I looked up at Regan and Skylar clutching each other as they stood on the sofa.

'There's nothing to be scared of,' I said, wringing my hands.

'Yet...' said Lex in a deep voice, following me move towards the kitchen.

'What did they expect?' I hissed. 'They knew the score! They've seen the photos!'

Lex nodded, distracted by Mum's snack pile. 'Don't worry about them. Oh, cool, you have popcorn!' She poked around the packets and boxes on the counter. 'And gingerbread men!'

 'They're ginger*dead* men,' I pointed out. Mum had snapped them up and fixed the broken edges back together with blood-red icing.

'Zombie biscuits!' Lex said admiringly. 'Crumbs! Ha ha.' We toasted each other with body parts and crunched.

'When are you going to show us to our rooms?' said Skylar, poking her head into the kitchen and eyeing it with a curled lip. 'I assume you have a kettle? I will be boiling the water before I drink anything.' She gave a little shudder. 'This is worse than camping, Bella.'

I could have cheerfully strangled her. This whole thing was her idea!

'Yes, of course we do,' I sighed, pointing at the old oven. Mum's shiny copper kettle sat on top.

'Better switch it on, then,' snipped Skylar, disappearing back into the lounge. I raised my eyebrows and Lex covered her mouth as her shoulders shook.

'Would saying "please" once in a while kill her?' I said, but I filled it and switched it on. The light flickered and the old socket buzzed, but a cup of tea would actually be nice.

'Thank youuuu!' sang Lex. I toasted her with an empty mug.

'Come on then, Skylar,' I said, heading back in to them. 'I'll show you upstairs. You're in the same room as R...Regan, if that's OK, because...'

'As long as I have my own bathroom!'

said Skylar. 'I need my own private space!'

'You wouldn't want to bathe alone here,' said Lex in a scary low voice. 'You must stay together after dark, or bad things will happen.'

Everyone was silent for a long moment as we digested this, until Skylar rolled her eyes and said, 'You're so weird, Alexandrina.'

The house creaked as the wind whipped past particularly viciously. The rain beat down harder, and I started to worry about the gaps in the roof. Hopefully we wouldn't be flooded out.

Skylar folded her arms and marched back to the stairwell. 'Well? Are we going up?'

We walked the splintery staircase gingerly up to the first floor and I pointed out the fact that only one way, the left-hand passage, was verified safe. Earlier on, Bob had reported there was extensive woodworm, wet rot, dry rot and even evidence of deathwatch beetles, or *Xestobium rufovillosum*... as I dragged my eyes from the section of skirting I was pointing to, I realised my specialist knowledge of infestations was unappreciated. I could tell I'd lost my audience. They were milling off the other way, exclaiming at the blooms of coloured mould growing up the peeling wallpaper, screaming at the glassy-eyed stag's head hanging on the wall at a peculiar angle, poking at the

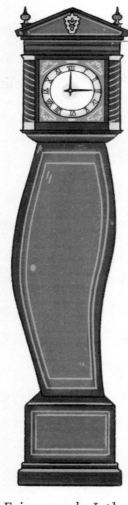

grandfather clock with the warped case. It was a weird clock, only chiming at six in the morning and midnight. So far it pretty much always managed to wake me up both times.

'In there.' I gestured awkwardly like some sort of waiter. Regan stared through the door and Skylar led her in.

It had been a pink-themed lady's room, long ago. Now it was a sad shadowy mess, but it was my room. Mum had made me promise not to let anyone use hers. *Fair enough*, I thought, as I watched them fight over who would get the bed and who would be on the floor beside the spooky black fireplace. Of course, Skylar won. Was it me or had I seen a look of annoyance cross Regan's face? I tried to imagine hanging out with Skylar every day and it made me want to scream. Lex and I backed out and looked at each other.

'We can share with them, dare to enter Mum's, or risk it in the next-door bedroom,' I said.

'Let's risk it with a biscuit in the next room,' said Lex, whipping out another gingerdead man and breaking the poor sucker in half. 'I bet Skylar snores. Heads or tails?'

I took the gingerdead head and beckoned her down the passageway. The blue room was OK, just not as clean as the pink one. I'd managed to sand the splintered wood and roll up a rug that had been sopping wet, for some reason. There was a four-poster bed in there, but only one you'd sleep on in a horror film. Instead of pretty lacy curtains it was festooned with cobwebs, and the idea of being the next meal of some hungry tarantula family did not appeal to me. 'We can take that corner.' I pointed, near the window.

Lex strolled across the creaky wooden floor and stared out at the gardens. 'You have a lot of land down there,' she said. 'The street lights edge it so prettily.'

'Hmm,' I said. 'See that messy wreck of stone over there?' I pointed far to the left. 'That's the old chapel you researched.'

'No way!' She shook her head. 'I wanted to sneak in to photograph it, but I didn't dare. I wish it wasn't raining. We could go and visit!'

'Oh... fun...' I said, suddenly glad of the rain.

We dumped our stuff and went back to check on the duo. They were still arguing over the bed.

'Why should I have the floor?' Regan was yelling. 'You're not the boss of me!'

I raised my eyebrows at Lex and we hurried past. Lex banged on their door and a chunk of soggy plaster dislodged and landed on her hair.

'Oh yuck!'

'Cup of tea anyone?' I called, and Lex and I ran down the stairs. In the kitchen, the kettle had boiled.

Skylar appeared next, asking for an organic hot chocolate, handing me a purple packet. Regan was behind her, her arms folded.

'I must say, Bella, I'm not keen on lying next to that fireplace thing in our room,' she said, leaning toward me.

'Why not?' I asked. 'It's just an original feature. All the rooms are creepy, Regan; we haven't had chance to decorate them yet, is all.'

'It's just that I saw... this.' She held up a small, dark red book. I eyed it, frowning. There was a golden insect design on the front, and the binding was frayed, like it was really old.

'Wait... where did you find this?'

'It was sort of hidden under the grate thing. I spotted it when I was laying out my sleeping bag. Look at the first page, Bella, and tell me you aren't creeped out.'

Slowly I opened the cover, and saw a torn front page. There was scrolling writing in faded brown ink, saying:

Compendium of Creeping & Crawling Creatures in Darkling Rectory by A.R.M.

It seemed to have been a collection of scientific drawings of insects, but some of it was ripped out. I looked at an ink drawing of a beetle for a long moment. 'I think that's a deathwatch beetle? It even shows the speckled detail. Just, wow.' I flipped the pages gently and stared at the creatures drawn inside.

Regan leaned over and shook her head at it. 'Wonder who A.R.M. was?'

'Well, whoever it was clearly lived here when the house was a rectory,' I said. 'That was from about 1750 until 1888, when the last vicar passed away. Mum does a *lot* of research on her house projects.'

Lex nodded. 'I remember the 1888 thing from my project. But I found in a library newspaper that he'd died of a broken heart due to his missing daughter.'

'Did you see the initials A.R.M. anywhere?' I asked. Lex shook her head.

I tried to smile at the others, but when I caught Regan's eye, she just looked troubled. Carefully, I put the book on the side to show Mum when she came back. She loved the old things we found. I usually did too, but I didn't like touching it, for some reason.

To distract myself, I focused on the drinks. As I poured and stirred, I saw Skylar twitch her head at Regan and they disappeared back into the lounge.

'What's that about?' murmured Lex, already slurping her tea and nibbling another bit of bleeding gingerbread. Her mouth was turning red from all the icing. I thought about the note Regan had given me in science and swallowed. There was no way she could have faked that book, though; I knew that for sure. It was too perfect for the era, too unsettling.

'Let's dial a pizza for dinner,' Skylar said as I followed them into the lounge when the drinks were ready, handing her the best mug Mum and I owned. She took a sip and pulled a face. 'Your water tastes dirty.'

I sighed. 'It's the s...same water that you get in the village!'

'Yeah, but your taps are filthy.'

I rolled my eyes and concentrated on my own drink. 'The sink has been scrubbed. Also, I don't have any m...money for pizza,' I said after a hot gulp to steady myself.

'I can afford it,' said Skylar, waving two twenties in the air. 'Dad was heading off with his new girlfriend to Chamonix, and he obviously felt guilty.' With a wicked smile she held up a hand to Regan, but I suddenly felt a bit sorry for her.

'We can't order it on my POOP app because none of our mobiles work in this *basic* place,' she went on. 'Have you got a landline, at least?'

'Your POOP app?' Lex looked puzzled.

'Yes,' snapped Skylar. 'POOP. It's obvious.'

'I'm not sure it is...' said Lex. Regan sniggered and Skylar glared at them both.

'Pizza Order-Out Prices.'

'What?' Regan snorted. 'You never told me you called it that!'

'It's easy to remember!' Skylar stamped her foot. 'Just shut up already. Now where is your telephone, Bella?'

'Right there,' I said, pointing at the vintage telephone on the floor by the long window.

Skylar moved across to it and dialled directory enquiries. I flinched, realising that was an expensive call, wondering how I would break it to Mum when she got the next bill.

Then Skylar held the receiver and stared at it, before tapping the phone buttons again.

'This thing is faulty,' she said. 'All I can hear is the wind.'

'What?' I asked. 'But Mum used it this morning to ring her conference. It must be OK?' My mind raced. Could it be a crossed line? Maybe a wire had blown into the neighbour's, with the wind and all.

'Well, you try it!' said Skylar, rolling her eyes. She snorted as I stumbled with nerves when I walked over to take it from her.

'Dial 422 for the directory thing to get the village pizza number,' she said.

'You mean the POOP number.' Lex chuckled.

I held the receiver to my ear and felt the backs of my knees go numb as I heard an odd crackling, and then the whispering voice. The hairs on my arms stood up as I recognised it, the strange, high-pitched girl's whisper. It carried on as I pressed all of the numbers, and even banging the buttons that cut the line didn't stop it.

'Play my game,' the voice was whispering, over and over. 'Coming! Ready. Or. Not.'

10

I slammed down the phone in horror and turned to the others, my skin crawling.

'D...did you... hear that?'

Skylar waved her hand dismissively at me. 'Yeah, the wind! Blowing in my ear. Useless thing.'

I realised she hadn't heard the whisperer. Unless... Could it have been Regan or Skylar? Was this the plan? I tried to catch my breath as I saw they were all staring at me like I was crazy. Maybe I was! This whole thing was totally crazy. But... how could they have whispered in the same voice that I'd heard on the first day? And said the same things about playing games? They couldn't possibly have known that.

'What's wrong?' asked Lex uncertainly.

'Erm... nothing...' I said.

'Rubbish!' Skylar folded her arms. 'Why are you so scared? You heard something, didn't you?'

'Is this some sort of set-up?' asked Regan.

'You tell me!' I said, watching Skylar closely. Lex looked from me to them, and narrowed her eyes.

'Let's stop with the tricks, right?' she said. 'This place is spooky enough.'

'Tricks?' said Skylar, trying for innocent but just looking devious. She nudged Regan. 'Who is playing tricks?' Regan gave a small, confused smile and shrugged her shoulders.

A long awkward moment passed until I stood up to sort out a carpet picnic in the lounge with the rest of the stuff Mum had left. 'W...we can't get pizza, but we have some snacks.'

After crisps and more crisps, we moved on to popcorn and sweets, and mugs of lemonade.

'I wonder if we'll get any trick-or-treaters?' said Lex with a burp. 'There's nothing left to give them!'

Skylar was sarcastic. 'Trick or treat? They'll never come here. It's like the world's worst building site! They'd be scared the whole place would blow down on them in this weather!'

We all fell quiet as the wind raced around, tapping those creepy branches on the windows again. The rain lashed on and off and I got the strangest feeling that we were on a boat, sailing into a storm. Around us, the house clanked and buzzed, cold and damp. The old lights above us trembled and flickered hazily in time with the wind.

My gaze fell onto the telephone, and I frowned. Whose voice had been on it? How was that even possible? Was it a ghost, here at Darkling?

I looked around at everyone and felt fireworks burst in my stomach as I realised that they were at *my* house, at *my* sleepover. I had friends for the first time... ever. I wondered again for a second if I should tell them about the whispers, but decided to keep it quiet for now at least. I wanted them to like me, not be scared of me.

Skylar stuffed a fistful of popcorn in her mouth. 'I can think of something far better to do than wait around for non-existent trick-or-treaters.' She glanced at Regan, raising her eyebrows as if encouraging her to do something, and then stood up. 'What we should do is have a little fun!'

I looked at Lex, who shoved her glasses up her nose, shaking her head at Skylar's bossiness.

'What sort of fun?' asked Regan, like she was reading from a script.

'Why, the perfect kind of fun for a house like this,' said Skylar, casting her arms wide and twirling around dramatically. I swallowed hard.

'Something we all used to play when we were kids,' she went on. She nodded at me, waiting for me to guess, but I just stared back at her.

She smiled, and loudly announced: 'Hide and seek...'

The rest of Skylar's words were swallowed by the floor lurching beneath her feet as the whole house shifted.

I screamed, falling against Lex, who banged her head on the arm of the sofa. There was a moment of weightlessness, and then the house resettled, dust puffing up all around us through all of the gaps and holes in the floor and walls.

'What was that?!' yelled Skylar, leaping up from the floor, where she'd landed.

'Was it an earthquake?' asked Regan, her eyes huge. 'This is mad! I've never been in an earthquake before!'

'Or is this whole place collapsing?' asked Lex quietly in my ear. 'You know... subservience? Subsidy?'

'Subsidence,' I whispered, standing up slowly, looking around me in amazement. I'd never known anything like it before. How could a whole house shift like that? Everything was safe, wasn't it? Bob had been here earlier! I took some deep breaths to calm down. I pictured the plans of the house and the huge cellar beneath us, trying to reassure myself that we wouldn't all end up collapsing into it. Then I froze. The voice chose that moment to whisper in my ear again and I had to fight to stop myself screaming.

'Ready or not...' it sighed tonelessly again. 'The game has been called!'

I looked around in shock. There was somebody here!

'I've fixed the doorsssss,' came a final whisper, and I jerked my head around. My ear was cold. I rubbed it, fingers icy with terror. Deep down I knew that there was nobody else here. And that the voice I'd just heard was **THE** voice. The front-door whisperer. The telephone 'winds'. I saw the school secretary's face as she told me about no previous family feeling happy here. Lex and Mum and their research – dead vicars and missing daughters. But that was... impossible. That was in the 1800s! I could almost feel how pale I'd gone – surely someone would notice! A swirl of panic bloomed in my chest. What was going on here?

'The house is perfectly... safe...' I muttered, but Lex stared at me, unconvinced.

My mind was racing. This was just all... too weird.

'I don't like earthquakes. I think I want to go home,' Regan wailed, and we watched as she bolted out of the room.

'Me too!' said Skylar, panic all over her, as she raced behind Regan to the front door. Lex and I caught up as they heaved on the handle, but the door wouldn't move.

'How do you... open this thing?!' Regan was screeching, her dark eyes massive in her face.

'Here,' I said, reaching for the handle.

'It's pretty heavy.' With a yank I tried to pull it open, but it wouldn't budge.

'What...?' I said. I tried again, but it was stuck fast. I scratched my head. There was nothing wrong with the door, was there? I thought of the whisper and 'I've fixed the doorsssss.'

'How can it be stuck?' I said, as Lex passed me the large key.

'Try unlocking it?' she asked, and I stuck it into the lock. It wouldn't move. She added her hands to mine, and we strained and yanked at different angles and depths. We worked on it for ten minutes, as Regan tried to breathe herself out of a panic attack and everyone's faces grew greyer.

'Have you got another way out?' asked Skylar finally, and I looked at her, trying to catch my breath from lock-wrestling. Her face was different when she was scared. It was like I could see a different girl underneath, now she'd stopped showing off and flouncing about.

'Well...' I said.

'Well what?'

'There is a back door. But it is also locked. And we don't have a key.' I shuffled about, thinking that this was starting to look bad. I crouched and peered through the keyhole, trying to be logical. The front door did have a history of odd behaviour. It had pushed me out, opened by itself, slammed itself, even though technically that was upwards and against gravity...

'Show me the back door!' demanded Skylar, and I took her past the kitchen and beyond the dining room, over to the other side where the original library had been, and the glass house.

The back door was completely warped into its frame. Mum had hired a specialist firm to come and sort it out but they couldn't come for another two weeks, and after more pushing and pulling we admitted defeat, trooping back to the lounge. Regan sat on the sofa, a dull look in her eyes.

'So,' said Skylar. 'You're telling me that there are only two doors out of this place and that both are locked or broken or faulty or whatever. That your telephone doesn't work.'

'And none of our mobile phones work properly,' said Regan, pulling hers out again and stroking it reverently.

'So we're *stuck*? Here?' Skylar's voice was getting higher. 'We'll have to smash a window!'

'No way,' I said. 'Have you seen them? They're t...too small. Plus they're solid leaded glass. Heavy and way too expensive to smash.'

'My father will pay for any damage,' said Skylar. 'He will fly back home directly once I tell him about all this. Or if we get hurt in here then Regan's dad will sue you, Bella, and your mother for leaving us here, all alone.'

I stared at her and thought of the lengths she'd gone to get in here. I felt cold fury filling up my insides.

'Shut up, Skylar,' I said. 'My mum will be back at midnight and I'm sure we'll be just fine until then. Or are you *scared* now?' For once my voice was clipped and strong, and inside I felt a satisfaction that I could stand up to her, if I had to.

Lex stared at me, and then nudged me with her elbow, murmuring, 'You don't need me here to protect you at all, do you? Way to go!'

I felt my face turning red, but I stood tall and kept my glare on Skylar.

There was an awkward silence.

'But what if there's a fire?' carried on Skylar.

'Well actually,' I said, 'we don't need to worry.' They all stared at me. 'I mean, we are stuck, but there might be another way out.'

'Oh, now she tells us!' said Skylar.

Regan perked up and looked at me. 'Where?'

'Follow me,' I said. I led them past the stairs and the other way, towards a hideous little parlour where Mum had started painting one wall, the other half filled with a collection of dead stuffed animals.

'Gross!' I heard somebody whisper.

'Here,' I said, my voice wobbling as I showed

them the arched black door that was set deep into the wall. *Halloween!* I thought suddenly. Is that why the voice wanted to play games? I remembered how cold my ear had turned when the whispers had happened, and I began to feel scared about tonight. Properly scared, like a heavy sense of dread had settled on me like a huge snake. It wrapped around my neck and tightened my throat.

'What is this?' demanded Regan, her eyes all big and hopeful. 'You never showed us this door! Where does it go?'

'It could be a way out.' I tried hard to sound sing-songy and positive. 'I've not been in, myself, but there are some small passages. They are on the plans of the house.'

Lex reached forward and turned the handle. Unlike the other doors in the house, the lock slid back easily, and the door fell open away from us. We stared down a flight of steep and cobweb-coated steps that disappeared into utter darkness.

'But... that's the cellar!?' squeaked Regan.

'And maybe a way out,' I said again, swallowing hard. 'I think...'

Skylar grabbed the door and slammed it shut. 'There's no way in hell any of us are ever going down there,' she said, her arms folded and her eyes twitchy. We looked at each other and then turned back to the lounge, moving slowly.

'Girls,' Skylar said at last, 'we're stuck here.' She closed her eyes and took a deep breath through her nostrils. After a moment, I saw she looked more like herself again. Sort of sharp, and with narrowed eyes. 'And this is a sleepover *party*, remember?'

Regan nodded, as Lex and I glanced at each other.

'So maybe instead of freaking out over a broken door we should have some fun, you know, and pass the time. Maybe we should play hide and seek?'

Two strange things happened as soon as she said those words. The house seemed to ripple again, like the light everywhere warped. Or was it just the dodgy electrics? I blinked hard. And then:

'Ready or not!' came the whisper, louder this time, and I jumped like a startled cat.

'Did you hear that?!' I yelled, and everyone looked at me, eyes like saucers.

'I think... I think I did!' said Regan, swallowing hard. 'Did someone whisper?'

'Oh for goodness' sake!' hissed Skylar. She whirled around to face me, and stamped her foot.

'This ISN'T funny, Bella! I *know* you're doing all of this stupid stuff for Halloween. Ooh!' She wagged her hands. 'We can't escape! All the doors are locked and the windows are fixed shut.' She banged a fist into the cellar door. 'The only way out, allegedly, is the creepiest staircase in the world.' She rolled her eyes. 'I know what you're doing, Bella, and you too, Lex! But I thought better of you, Regan.' She leaned towards Regan, sparks flying out of her eyes. Regan backed into the wall.

'I'm on to you all,' Skylar said, moving her mouth slowly. 'So now we'll all play *my* game.'

I goggled at her, not knowing what to say. She thought *we* were playing a Halloween joke?

'You count,' said Skylar to me, standing up on her toes and stretching her arms high. 'OK. Come on, everyone. This'll be fun and totally take our minds off this crazy situation.'

'Hold on. You think *we* are doing this?' asked Regan, pointing at me, Lex and herself. 'In this earthquake house? Are you mad!?' Her voice was screechy. 'Prisoners!' She shook her head. 'Seriously, are the electrics even safe here?' She looked at me for a beat. 'Do you even *have* electrics?'

'Yes, we do have electrics. How do you think the lights are working?' I pointed upwards and, unhelpfully, the lights flickered off for a second. I scowled. 'And *yes*, they are safe. Most of them, anyway.' Upstairs was quite another matter. Another thing on Bob's snagging list, to be honest. Skylar and Regan raised an eyebrow at each other.

'OK,' I said hastily. I needed to save this situation. Prove I wasn't a total sleepover failure.

Maybe it wasn't too late. 'A game might be fun. I'll seek – I'm counting to a hundred.' I swallowed. We were all here together... it was fine. Everything was going to be fine. My heart was thundering a little too fast in my chest.

Skylar grabbed Regan's hand and dragged her off, and Lex raised her eyebrows at me as she darted off in another direction. I counted slowly, trying to persuade myself that yes, this could actually be fun. I heard feet running overhead, and wished I'd reminded them to avoid the unsafe right-hand side of the first floor. I tried to focus on Mum saying that the whole place was basically sound. Victorian buildings, Bob always said, over and over. Safe as houses. Then I remembered the strange wobble-earthquake that the house had done when Skylar said about playing hide and seek. And the second wobble when Skylar had said... Wait! The house had shaken from its foundations when the words 'hide and seek' were said. But why? My brain seemed to be stuck in treacle.

Some dust fell from the ceiling like dandruff as they scampered about. I sped up the counting a little, not wanting them to hide in places too hard to find. I paused around seventy-one as I heard the back door rattle, and a few whispers. Who was trying to go outside? I sat up tall, leaning forward and straining my ears. They evidently gave up, as feet came lightly running back past the lounge door, and I couldn't help but smirk, shaking my head. They'd be easy to find.

'Coming!' I yelled. 'Ready or not!' As I hollered the words I went cold, remembering the whispering voice repeating the same thing. At the door I paused, looking right towards the kitchen and left to the front door. Where would they be? I froze, listening to the house. It was so big, there were lots of tiny sounds that my ears honed in on.

I closed my eyes and mentally roamed around. There was creaking from the dining room, footsteps overhead, a muffled thump from somewhere on the landing, and the wind and rain buffeting around the edges of the house.

I tiptoed into the kitchen first, checking everything. There was nowhere to hide in there, but I passed into the dim utility area, which was to become a wet room. Nothing was there yet but our second-hand washing machine. I looked glumly at the clothes in the basket in front of it and remembered that Mum had asked me to do some washing. Then I frowned, as I realised the washing looked a bit... jumbled, somehow. *No time now*, I thought. The back door was still warped closed, and I passed across into the dining room with the shadowy doors into the Victorian glass house. It made my skin crawl, that filthy place. It stank of pondweed and was ankle-deep with tangled roots and the husks of long-dead insects. I couldn't imagine anyone would've hidden in there, but it seemed more logical to check all of the ground floor first. I peered through the mossy glass into the green-tinted darkness and had the shock of my life when a face thrust forwards on the other side.

I jerked back, smacking my hip on the old dining table, clapping a hand over my mouth to hold in a scream.

'Surprise!' said Lex, opening the glass door gingerly. I stared at her for a moment, feeling relief flood through me and blowing out a deep breath.

'You scared me to death!' I said, pressing a hand to my chest to reassure myself.

'The moths in there are unreal,' she said, thumbing backwards towards the glass house again. 'Do you know what they study in school?'

'School?' I blinked. 'I don't know?'

'Mothmatics.' She started to laugh, and after a moment I joined in.

'I love them,' she said. 'When I was little, Mum got me caterpillars to hatch into butterflies every year. Seeing them all flitting off in the garden was brilliant!'

I shook my head at her. 'I just had a calculator to practise working out paint and wallpaper quantities.'

She grinned. 'Useful! Height multiplied by

width. Speaks *volumes* about your mum, ha! Suppose we'd better go and find the others?'

I sighed. 'We probably should.'

'Or we could leave them a while!'

'We could, actually.' I was laughing with her now. 'We could just say they were really great at hiding!' I was glad she was here. Deeply glad.

We wandered back through the kitchen, helping ourselves to some of the chocolate biscuits and a quick glass of lemonade.

'Right,' said Lex, hiccupping. 'Where are they likely to be?'

I shrugged. 'There are so many places.'

'How many bedrooms?'

'Six on the first floor, three huge ones on the second, attics above those. Over the unsafe part is the clock tower.'

'So there are... nine bedrooms?' Lex looked amazed. 'Finding the duo could take ages!'

'One of the big ones is locked,' I said. 'So they can't be in there.'

'Locked? Why?'

'No idea. It was the original master suite, Mum says. The door's a proper antique, all hand-carved oak with rabbits and leaves and stuff. Anyway, the thing has immense value, which means nobody can smash the lock.'

'This house and its doors,' muttered Lex. 'It doesn't want us to escape!'

Her joke fell flat as I thought again about the front door, and the 'doorsssss' whisper. 'I'm going to try it again when we go past,' I said. 'It is a weird door, but it's never actually jammed before. Bob even oiled it, earlier. How is Mum going to get in when she gets back?'

'What time is she due?' asked Lex.

'Just after midnight.' I checked my watch. It was almost eight o'clock.

I felt a sudden crawling feeling in my stomach. 'I hope neither of them has tried to climb up the clock tower. It hasn't been checked since around 1903.'

13

We moved steadily past the lounge again and the miserable grey sitting room. We poked our heads in but I could see from the thick dust on the floor that nothing had moved in there. Anyone walking in would have left footprints. It was freezing cold and Lex shivered. 'This house is so full of delights.'

I nodded. I was used to living in decrepit old ruins, but she wasn't. We made it to the front door, and I tried to turn the key. It was no good. Almost like something in the mechanism had snapped and jammed. I tried to tell myself it was that, a real physical lock failure and not something a whispering voice was able to do. 'Mum's going to be cross,' I observed, and put the key back by the ugly vase.

She stopped and stared at me. 'Hold up. You are doing all this aren't you?' she breathed. 'As a Halloween party trick. The doors jamming, the telephone! How are you making the house wobble, though? Brilliant!'

'No, I'm not,' I said. She winked at me.

'I'm not!' I shook my head. 'I swear. I half-thought it was Skylar and Regan's joke... you know, the note?'

'I know Skylar has resources and too much money at her disposal, but I don't see how they could have organised even the telephone thing.' Lex frowned and whipped her glasses off to polish them.

The other way past the front door led through what we'd called the front parlour, where Mum had been testing different jewel-coloured wallpapers. The floor was oak, and she'd sanded a large corner of it. Lex paused. 'You can see how amazing the place is going to look!'

I nodded, feeling a whoosh of pride at Mum's

skills. The other half of the room was draped in dust sheets, but against the walls we could see cabinets filled with evil-eyed stuffed animals. The door at the rear led to the oak-panelled study, and a small library.

'It's like Cluedo!' Lex exclaimed as we wandered through. 'It was me, in the study, with a candlestick.' There were a few water-damaged books on the dark wood shelves, and she picked one up.

'*The Gentleman's Handbook*,' she read, her eyes wide.

I pulled a face. 'It'll be all about how to manage a household by controlling your wife and offspring.'

'It literally is,' she said, shaking her head. '*A Happy Household in the Hands of Any Gentleman*,' she read. 'Not exactly what us independent young women want to be reading.' She slid it back onto the shelf.

'Maybe the young woman of the time was busy writing that insect book,' I said lightly, thinking about the elegant, scrolling handwriting, and Lex nodded.

'The mysterious A.R.M. Can I borrow it, actually?'

'Sure. Hmm, I bet there's a secret passage,' I said. 'Mum was showing me there's something odd noted around here on the plans. She said sometimes these old houses had hidden rooms.'

'A secret wall?' asked Lex, pressing and pushing on the library shelves in a frenzy. After a moment I joined in, but nothing opened or shifted. Disappointed, we turned back and walked to the foot of the stairs again.

'They must both be up there.' I stared up, noticing a large cobweb with a fat black spider crouching in the middle.

We listened hard. I was hoping for some noise to help pinpoint them, but all was quiet.

I nodded at Lex and we started up, slowly and as carefully as we could. The stairs were old and shabby, but solid, and apart from occasional damp carpet treads squishing underfoot, they didn't make much sound as we climbed. At the top we breathed and listened again. I peered nervously to the right where the floors were untested and hoped they hadn't gone around there. Lex moved along the passageway and leaned into the duo's own bedroom, but aside from a mountain of make-up and hair products, it was empty.

'Too obvious,' she whispered. We advanced to our room. I looked in this time, and again saw nothing but our sleeping bags.

'All quiet,' I mouthed. Next along the passage was the small bathroom where the plumber had startled Lex, and we both peered in. There wasn't room for a cat to hide in there.

There still wasn't a peep from either of the duo. I started to get a tinge of worry.

'Where would they hide?' I murmured to myself.

Mum's room was next, locked but with the key in the door. I tried the handle and was irritated that it glided open, meaning some cheeky person had unlocked it. I gestured for Lex to look left, while I went right around the bed and headed towards the old wardrobe. With a snap I yanked open the doors, and jumped to see Regan in there, covered in one of Mum's sheets, holding up her phone. The flash pinged and blinded me, as she **WOOOOOO**ed and leapt out, stretching her arms up. 'I'm a ghost! Surprise! Blimey, I've been in there for ages! Have I won?'

I blinked my eyes back to normal and stared at her. 'Did you take that out of the laundry basket?'

Regan pulled the sheet off and shook her curls back. 'It was Skylar's idea,' she said, looking at her feet. 'At least I stopped her cutting eye-holes in it. I tried to warn you...'

'So she was planning to try and freak me out!' I nodded at Lex, who raised her eyebrows.

Regan shrugged. 'Anyway, did I win?'

I blew out my cheeks. 'Sorry, but we're still looking for Skylar.'

'So *she* won!' she said. 'Typical. I'll come with you guys.'

I shut the wardrobe when she was out of the way, after straightening Mum's trainers and a spare high-vis jacket. I left the sheet on the floor, reminding myself to move it before Mum got back. I was glad Regan had stopped Skylar cutting it. After we exited the room, I carefully locked the door again.

'It's good to be out of there!' she said, stretching again.

'That was my mum's room,' I said, scowling at her. 'It was locked for a reason!'

She shrugged. 'That's why I thought it would be a good hiding spot. I didn't touch anything, I promise.'

I sniffed the air, my eyes narrowing. 'That's Mum's perfume!'

'Sorry...' Regan looked sheepish. 'I only had a tiny spray.'

Lex shook her head.

Backing away from Mum's room at last, I looked along the passageway and cursed to myself. Skylar was obviously in one of the harder to reach areas. 'Stay by the edges,' I hissed to them, and we began to traverse the untested half of the first floor. There was a huge lilac bedroom, I tried to think, a green one, and then a yellow one, which had hideous damp. With three of us looking it was faster to clear those rooms, even though they were far bigger than the bedrooms we were staying in.

'Why couldn't we sleep in these?' asked Regan.

The yellow one looked like the walls were crying. It was horrible. 'Because none of them are safe!' I said. 'If someone went crashing through a ceiling, Mum would be furious. And said person would likely break a leg. Or their neck.'

Regan fell quiet.

Back at the stairs, I pointed up. The second-floor bedrooms were up there, all as big as the lilac suite, but neither Mum nor I had been in since Mum first looked over the place to sign the renovation contract with Mrs Hallorann. We tiptoed up, and

I noticed how the floor just off the stairs felt all weird and off-balance.

'It's not level!' said Lex, swooping down a rise in the floor.

'Careful!' I said.

'It feels like we're on a bouncy castle!' said Regan, who suddenly seemed a lot more fun without Skylar around. We took a moment to tiptoe up and down the wobbles.

I tried the first door and looked into a dark room stuffed with broken furniture.

'Found you,' I whisper-called, hoping if Skylar was there she would give up graciously.

'Have you got a torch?' asked Regan, and I thought a moment. There was one, somewhere. Candles were a bad idea in a house with so much wood. I tried to think where Mum would've left her torch as Lex and Regan moved broken chairs and a cracked mirror around to look for Skylar. After ten minutes, we gave up. Regan shone the torch from her phone, but said her battery was running out so she flicked it off.

The second bedroom on the right was completely empty, with black smoky marks up one wall, likely from a small fire. It looked like nobody had been in for about a hundred years so I closed the door with a shudder. The third one was the one with the hand-carved antique door, which I knew was locked with a foreign body jammed in the mechanism. Mum had been waiting for the guys who were fixing the back door to come and advise us on how best to open it. As we gathered together to discuss our next move, Regan leaned on the handle and lost her balance as it swung open.

'What the...?' I said, my mouth wide open. 'That's... impossible!'

14

Regan clambered up off the floor and dusted off her elbows. 'Ouch.'

'The doors here are all backwards!' said Lex. 'The ones that should open don't, and the ones that shouldn't all do!' She followed Regan in as I tried to find my breath and tell them to wait.

The four-poster bed was strangely perfect, the engraved frame matching the door. It was huge, made of chunky brown wood.

'Mum'll be thrilled with this,' I said, running my fingers down the exquisite carvings. There were yellowed sheets on the bed, which were thick with dust, and a huge black fireplace. Lex moved to the small bay window and I followed, staring out at the front of the house. The whole street was visible as it gently advanced down the hill. I took comfort in the street lights and the houses around us. There was a whole world of people out there, all going about their normal lives. If I strained my eyes, I could even see tiny torches bobbing around the streets as groups of children trick-or-treated, despite the rain. Everyone else was enjoying a normal Halloween, and Mum would be catching her train home soon. Everything would be OK.

Behind us there was a rustle and a hand burst out from under the bed. We all jumped like we'd been electrocuted, and I let out a loud scream.

'What the?!' shrieked Lex.

'It's Skylar!' said Regan.

'How did you unlock the door?' I demanded as she rolled out athletically and dusted herself off.

'What are you talking about? It was open!' she said. 'And your *Alice* was here with me too, but I sent her to find you after we got bored.

Was this part of your plan to freak us all out? Well, it didn't work on me. I wasn't scared at all.' She looked at Regan. 'Did you do the sheet thing? Did you get a good picture?'

'Yes,' said Regan, catching my eye and blushing.

We all stared at each other.

'Hold on here,' I said. 'Wait a second. Someone was *with* you?' I suddenly felt all loose and weird, like my body was giving way.

'Yes,' Skylar snapped, as if I was stupid. 'You must have passed her.'

'B...but... did you say *Alice*?' I said again, my voice crackling. My stomach rolled.

'Duh!' said Skylar. 'Why don't you try listening! *Yes*, Alice. She said she knew you really well. That she knew you would love to play her game... and that she told you all about the doors. She told me the doors here played tricks on her so she controls them now. I think she was joking? But, Bella, really. I can't actually believe that you didn't tell us your flipping best friend would be here.'

Regan sneezed in the small dust cloud she'd created.

I sat on the bed. 'She knows me... *really well*?' My brain started fizzing. The doors? Playing the game? Was Alice the whisperer?

'She was going on about how she liked the hiding better than the seeking,' said Skylar. 'She hates seeking.'

Lex frowned at me. 'You never said you had a friend here?'

I put my head in my hands. 'That's because I don't.'

'What?' Skylar blinked at me. 'Who was she, then? She was a bit older than us, I think.'

I folded my arms. Alice!? I felt a sharp pain in my stomach. What was happening here? This didn't make sense. How could this Alice know me really well, and whisper in my ear without even being in the same room? How could she commandeer a telephone?

They all looked at me, waiting for an explanation. I started to get hot.

I tried to think up an excuse. 'She... ah, she used to live here.'

There was a beat of silence as everyone seemed to consider this.

'Ah. And then you and your mum came, and she had to move out.' Skylar brushed dust off her designer top.

'Sort of,' I said. 'But she... doesn't want to go.'

'Where are her family?' asked Lex, who still looked baffled.

'They're all... dead.' I said. Everything was spinning out of control. Why was I making up this stupid story?

'Dead?' Regan shook her head. 'That's so sad.'

'Yes,' I said slowly.

'But you didn't see her? She must have walked right past you?' said Skylar. 'She had this hideous brown dress on. I thought she was dolled up for Halloween, you know.'

'Er, no,' said Lex as my mind raced. We could have missed her, as we'd been ducking in and out

125

looking in all of the rooms. But if she was trying to find us, surely she would have heard us talking?

Skylar rolled her eyes. 'Now we'll have to declare her the winner.'

'Yes,' I said. 'But where is this... Alice now?'

15

We left the large suite and trooped downstairs. I couldn't believe that Alice was a real girl, and was almost jealous that Skylar had clearly seen her. I had heard her whisper in my ear, and speak on the telephone, but now she was *here*? What was going on? Who was she? Was it her that had made the house shake twice? Did she really want to play hide and seek with us? Why didn't she like seeking? The more I thought, the more confused I became. And why had she told Skylar she knew me really well?! That gave me a nasty stab of terror.

'*Was* that your friend?' Lex whispered to me. 'Or is something very strange happening here?'

'I don't know anyone called Alice, except for

the girl Skylar just told us about. I swear!' I stared at her.

Lex didn't have any jokes about that. 'So what was all the stuff about her having lived here, and her dead family?'

I shrugged miserably. 'I had to try and explain somehow. You know as much as me!'

I replayed the bedroom conversation as we went back to the kitchen for a drink. Skylar washed her hands in the sink to get the dust off, and Lex quietly nibbled the last gingerdead man.

Then there was the question of what Alice was up to. She was in here with us, somewhere, so what was she doing right now? I cocked my head and listened, but I could just hear Lex and Regan opening more packets of biscuits.

'Skylar,' I said carefully. 'What did Alice look like? Er, to you, I mean?'

She stared at me like I was mad. 'You're

seriously asking me what *your* secret Halloween surprise friend looks like?'

I froze, unable to answer. 'Erm, I mean... d... did she look... OK?'

'Is this all part of a hilarious master plan of a joke you're playing on us?' asked Skylar in a flat tone. 'And I've ruined it all for you?' She shook her head, not waiting for my answer. 'You had your mate Alice hidden, ready to jump out at us and scare us to death. Well, all I can say is you need friends who are cleverer at tricks. Am I right, Regan?'

We all looked around, but she wasn't in the kitchen.

Lex rapidly polished her glasses and then said, 'She was just right here!'

I stared around and walked back to the foot of the stairs. There was no sign of her.

'Has she gone to the loo?' asked Skylar, shaking her hands dry.

We all stood by the stairs and Skylar yelled

'RE-GAAAAAN!' at the top of her voice. We looked in every direction to see where she would appear.

A long moment passed, and then Skylar shouted again. 'REGAN! COME OUT NOW; DON'T BE SO ANNOYING!'

'Could she have gone exploring further?' asked Lex, pointing up. I stared up, thinking about all of the rooms up there, like the attics, huge dark spaces full of furniture and old paintings.

'Why would she have gone up when she was in the kitchen with us?' said Skylar, totally exasperated. 'I told her the rest of the joke was off. She should have...'

'Wait,' I said, frowning. 'The rest of the joke?'

'Oh!' said Skylar, widening her eyes innocently. 'It was nothing.'

'What was nothing?' said Lex, folding her arms.

'Nothing was nothing!'

'Nothing was clearly something.' Lex narrowed her eyes and walked about like Miss Marple.

'Come on, Skylar – it might help us figure out where Regan has got to.'

Skylar looked at the floor and folded her arms too.

'It was only a joke,' said Skylar. 'And we didn't even do it, anyway. Because there was only one sheet in the laundry basket, so she took that one, and then the doors didn't open.'

'What doors?' I asked, trying not to look as baffled as I felt.

'The *door* doors!' She rolled her eyes, but she looked slightly awkward without Regan backing her up.

'Explain yourself!' I yelled, clenching my hands into fists.

'Fine.' Skylar sniffed. 'When the game started and you were counting, we were going to put sheets on and run outside through the back door. And then bang on the windows.'

'But why? Just to scare us?' said Lex.

'And then haunt you. As real ghosts, in the house.

And get some photographs and videos of you all scared.'

I thought of Regan's note. I couldn't believe I had wasted one second worrying about it – especially after everything that had happened since. It was actually nice of Regan that she'd tried to give me a heads-up, I thought.

'I didn't take into account doors that didn't open,' scoffed Skylar, throwing her hands into the air. 'Or the lack of ghost dressing-up. The sheets on the beds were *way* too icky to put on. This whole place has more dust than a sandstorm. I thought you were pretending the back door didn't work just to scare us. So sue me.' Her blue eyes looked furious. 'What about your secret *Alice* friend?' she hissed. 'Maybe Regan has gone off with her somewhere.'

'Well, it doesn't explain where either of them have got to as the doors are still locked and stuck,' I said, scratching my nose. I didn't want to talk about Alice at all, because what kind of person has a sleepover with a strange guest even she doesn't know about? Ice trickled down my spine as I realised the idea of Regan following the mysterious Alice somewhere wasn't a nice one.

'All I wanted was a pizza,' said Skylar to nobody in particular. 'And to have a fun Halloween. I should have stayed at home.'

Lex caught my eye and offered me a smile of support. I stared at them both, annoyed that Skylar was complaining. This whole mess had been her idea.

'OK,' said Lex. 'Let's go and find Regan, and maybe Alice too, and then we can have some toast or something, right, Bella?'

I nodded. Sure. Toast would fix the lamest party in the history of history. I tried to put weird Alice out of my head and remember if we had any jam.

16

We looked for Regan around the ground floor, Lex taking the opportunity to try and find the secret library passage again. We held our faces close to the shelves, and Lex swore she could feel a breeze, but no amount of banging or tapping or pulling out books worked.

'Are you absolutely sure there's no other way out?' asked Skylar. I rolled my eyes.

Like we hadn't already been over this. 'Maybe the cellar,' I said with a shrug.

'She wouldn't have gone down there,' Skylar said after a moment. 'She's scared of the dark.'

'It's a smart thing to be scared of,' said Lex.

I stared at Skylar, the sharp little face downcast

now she'd lost her buddy. I realised that inside she was probably just as worried as me. I stood a bit taller, pushing my shoulders back. Darkling was my house, and Alice was my mysterious guest. As long as we stayed together to look for Regan, everything would be fine. I tried to tell myself that maybe the mystery would turn out to be an interesting Halloween sleepover after all.

Skylar goggled at me for a moment as she seemed to gather herself. 'Look, Bella, I swear. This isn't a joke. It isn't. And Regan, well, she's my friend. And I'm getting sort of worried about her. Now what about you and *your* joke? Who is this Alice?'

'Alice is just...' I tried to find the words.

'Regan has been missing for about forty minutes,' said Lex. 'We can't get out and ask for help, no phones work... what about email? Can we email the police?'

'Email the police?' Skylar closed her eyes.

'They'll think it's a Halloween prank,' I said. '"Dear police, please come to the spookiest house in the village where we've been playing Halloween hide and seek and we can't find our friend." They'll sit back and laugh their uniform socks off. Look, she's here somewhere. There are a lot of rooms.' I started thinking that maybe she'd gone somewhere dangerous and something had happened to her. But we hadn't heard any crumbling or crunching sounds, like when a ceiling gives way. Or any screams or shouts for help. I shivered. I certainly didn't want to hear any of those things, even though they would explain where she was. 'My mum says no news is good news,' I said. 'Everything will be fine. Let's go and look for her again, but this time, everywhere, OK?'

'There are more places?' Skylar asked.

'Yep. There's a whole clock tower it's possible to get to, although it's dangerous.'

'Oh my gosh, what if she's actually hurt?' said Skylar, a troubled look clouding her blue eyes.

'I did first aid at Brownies,' said Lex.

'Well, we're all safe now we have a *Brownie* here.'

Skylar eye-rolled. 'You can knit us a tea cosy. Come on, already!'

'I failed my knitting badge,' muttered Lex.

We lined up by the stairs. I held my fingers to my lips so we could listen hard for Regan, in case she was trying to get our attention from somewhere. There was nothing. The house seemed to stretch upwards, all dark, empty space. We crept up like mice on tiptoes, freezing at every tiny creak.

At the top of the stairs, Skylar asked if we should split up. Lex wrinkled her nose thoughtfully, and I folded my arms.

'We can cover more ground that way,' Lex said slowly, throwing in support for Skylar.

I shook my head. 'Too many floors here are unsafe. If you're not with me, how will you know where to take extra care?'

'Fine.' Skylar pouted. 'Let's get on with it. REGAN!' she yelled so suddenly we all jumped. There was a scurrying sound on the passageway and we all sprang backwards, fearing a mouse or a rat, but instead a large black moth bashed its way around the corners of the high ceilings.

'It's a death's-head hawk-moth! Extra creepy because it's Halloween,' said Lex, tucking her arm in mine. I nodded, admiring the skull pattern on its body. It looked huge, swooping and crashing around. I couldn't help ducking my head as we edged past, imagining it tangled in my hair.

We steadily worked higher and higher, until a furious bellow from behind stopped us dead.

'What's wrong?' I asked, my heart hammering. I jogged a few steps back to Skylar, trying to breathe normally.

'It's finally all clear.' Skylar was waving her arms around, and I was shocked to see a tear glisten in her eye. 'She's playing a joke on *me*!' She stamped her foot like a petulant toddler, and I blinked at her in shock. 'All the years that I've known her, all the things I've done. I've been an *amazing* friend to her!'

'You mean Regan?' I asked.

'Yes. My so-called best friend.' She hissed the word though her teeth, and I took a step back. I looked at Lex to say something, anything to help. She shrugged at me, helpless. Everything around us was quiet. I tuned Skylar's tantrum out and started to get a bad feeling about Regan. We jumbled position as Skylar went ahead, and I followed her along the passageway, peeking in through the doors, looking for Regan's footprints in the thick dust coating most of the rooms' carpets. There was no sign of anyone.

Skylar turned to look at us, a smudge of grime on her nose. She cocked her head sideways at something behind me and gasped.

'What?'

'Lex has gone!'

17

'What?' I repeated, a sinking sensation in my stomach that felt uncomfortably like someone had just pulled a plug out somewhere at the bottom. 'You're messing.' I turned all the way around, realising Lex had indeed disappeared. 'She was just here! Like a second ago!' I held my arms out in shock.

'I am not messing!' Skylar's voice was getting shrill. 'Are you all involved? Is this a total mockery of me? Because you're jealous or something? In all my days I have never...'

'Neither Lex nor I are involved in anything,' I said in a dangerous voice. 'Don't you dare accuse us of something when the only one planning stupid ghost jokes was *you*!' I stared her down until

Skylar's face crumpled and she began to sob noisily.

'How could they do this to me?' she wailed. 'I'm a good friend!'

'I don't think they have purposely...' I said, but now I was feeling doubtful. First Regan, now Lex too? They were messing about. They had to be! I scowled at Skylar. Was she just tricking me too? Crying crocodile tears to make me feel scared? I examined her face. There was snot pouring from her nose and she snorted and wiped it roughly with the back of her hand. Her upset was real, I decided. Nobody could be that disgusting an actress.

We stood huddled in the upstairs passageway, unsure of what to do next. I had a sudden terrible suspicion. Could this *all* be something to do with this strange Alice?

Then came a sound from downstairs.

'What is *that*?' said Skylar in a funny high-pitched voice. It sounded like some sort of music. I strained my ears to listen. The slightly off-key piano scales. My skin tingled.

'Is it them?' she gurgled. Without another word, she turned and ran back down.

'Wait!' I said, but after a moment I knew that I had no choice but to chase after her, my heart jumping like a frog in my chest. Skylar must have run very fast, because I couldn't catch her.

'Skylar?' I called through the hallway in a soft voice. But there was no sign of her. 'Where did she go?' I was talking to myself, but I was too freaked out to care.

It was like she'd vanished into thin air, and I began to feel queasy. 'What's happening?' I whispered. There was a strange smell in the air, and I sniffed it as I walked towards the lounge, where the door was shut.

'Have you gone in there?' I asked nobody. I held out my hand in slow motion and leaned to twist the door handle. It felt icy cold in my hand, cold enough to burn, and I yelped in shock, letting go and shoving my hand under my arm.

But what kind of music was this? As the door

slowly opened, I could hear a simple tune being hammered out on a piano that wasn't in the house. I let out a tiny moan. It was like my feet had locked to the floor, and I couldn't move a muscle. Then I realised that I could see my breath, it was so cold. I started to shake then, all my muscles twitching and trembling.

I stared around as my throat tightened. I squeaked when the door slowly creaked open by itself and I spotted a triangular wedge of the room, which looked oddly colourless, like a black and white film. Was I getting a migraine? I squeezed my eyes shut to try and find my normal vision. But when I opened them again, it didn't alter the dark grey cast of the room. I jumped when I saw a white oval straight ahead, and it took a long second before I recognised my own reflection. My face in the mirror was all wide mouth and eyes. My scalp was contracting, as if my skin was shrinking.

There was no sign of Skylar, Regan or Lex. Instead, as I took a faltering step inside, I got a whiff of smoke, and stared in amazement at a piano that had appeared in the corner of the room.

'*What...?*' I whispered, not believing my eyes.

How did that get there? I stared at it, trying to hold my chattering teeth still and taking a deep breath of musky air. A *baby grand* piano, I thought in amazement, its lid propped open. That's what it was. Shining like a conker. Mum had a couple of historical books for the houses we worked in, and I'd seen one in there. My mind was working in slow-motion as I tried to compute one here, before me. Where on earth had that come from? Then something whooshed across from the piano to the fireplace. I gasped, squeezing my eyes shut in fright.

'L...l...look...' I told myself, and I forced my eyes open, away from the instrument and over to the fireplace where there was something else different and odd and very, very impossible. I felt my stomach loosen again as I tried to croak something, tried to say anything, my brain fighting in vain to understand what was there, in the room in front of me.

'Urg...' I managed, trying to swallow.

For there, facing the window, was a figure. My brain slowly realised it must be the strange girl Skylar had met. *Alice!* I could not take my eyes off her. She wore the brown dress Skylar had mentioned, and had her hair parted and pulled into long dark plaits, thinner and sleeker than mine, tied with ribbons, the ends curling. They looked... damp? Her edges were misty. A moan escaped from me and I clenched my hands so tightly they ached.

She slowly turned her head and looked straight at me.

18

My whole body seized up like I had been flash-frozen into place. My teeth clenched together even harder as my brain urgently told me to get out of there.

She was grey-ish, like the odd light in the room, and also flickering in and out of focus like the piano. But as I watched, I saw her get stronger until she was right there with me, as real as I was. I shook my head, because this was impossible. A thousand feelings rushed through me like a waterfall.

Alice was here... but wasn't here... she was real... but not real. The room looked like a museum – like the past had become the present? Oh my... this was utterly crazy.

The room started to spin as my mind caught up

with what my eyes were seeing. Alice was from the past, and wasn't alive... she was a... *ghost*...? I tried to keep breathing as I considered this and stared at her in front of the fireplace. Utter terror was flowing through me like ice water.

The fire she stood by hadn't been lit, but somehow now there were orangey-grey flames jumping on the logs. My confused brain tried to figure it out and I stared at it, mesmerised, before pulling my eyes away and gazing back at her.

She was facing me now. Tall and thin, she was wearing a brown pinafore. Her feet were bare, and dirty. One of her legs was hanging at a strange angle below the knee. Something about her expression was absolutely awful.

'Are y...you r...real?' I whispered, and my eyes opened wide as I waited to see if she would answer.

Then she smiled at me. I jerked backwards at the sight of that smile. It was the most terrifying thing I'd ever seen. All I could think was that that smile was a bad thing pretending to look good.

'Practice makes perfect, Pa used to say. The piano belonged to Ma, so very long ago.' She sighed. 'I like knowing her fingers played the same keys.'

The words she spoke ran a little slower than her mouth appeared to move, which made it hard to hear, and I frowned as I concentrated on her.

'How nice that you have friends here for Halloween! I didn't really have any friends of my own, you know. Pa threw me a party one year for my birthday, but the girls found my compendium and were afraid of me after that. Elspeth and Verity tore it.'

I blinked at the word 'compendium', seeing the ripped pages in the red book in my mind's eye.

'So I caught a few creepies to scare them. Pa said I could never have a party again.'

'You... *scared* them?'

'And then I heard you and your friends at your little *party*, declaring a game of hide and seek. On Halloween eve of all nights, and it gave me an unusual strength.'

Gave her an unusual strength? Hide and seek? I remembered the odd vibration that the house had made, and I swallowed hard. My dry throat clicked. 'Did you... make the house *wobble*?'

'The house moves with me,' she went on. 'It shifts as I return.' She came closer, dragging her injured leg. I could feel the cold emanating from her. If I squinted I could even see it, a silvery haze like a frost that fizzed and spat around her outline.

She seemed to grow taller and leaned over me somehow, moving her face too close. I tried to shrink away but I couldn't. Her eyes were like swirling oceans of darkness.

'I live in this house, Bella, and you're all playing my game.'

'Your game?' I repeated in a tiny voice, as if all of my energy had flowed out of me like leaking water.

'I love hide and seek,' she said, the peculiar smile coming back, moving her mouth but darkening her eyes. I tried to look away from her, but I couldn't. 'I want to play it forever!'

I blinked, and she swirled into a mist for a moment, before reappearing even closer to me.

'Play *forever*?' I stammered.

'I was no good at seeking. Not that last time. I could not find... him. So this time I have—' Her eyes grew darker. 'I have hidden them. And if you don't find them, I get to keep them! And then they'll stay with me here, in Darkling! That's the best way the game can finish.' She cocked her head on one side. 'And I won't be alone any more!'

I looked wildly around the room as I felt my chest tighten. 'What do you mean?!' I shouted, badly scared now. 'You took Lex? And Skylar and Regan?'

Her face took on a gleeful expression.

'They're inside the house. But well-spaced apart!' She laughed then, a deathly giggle that hurt my ears so that I clamped my hands over them.

I had the crazy thought that this was all a terribly elaborate Halloween joke, orchestrated by Skylar and about to be released on the internet for a million people to laugh at me.

Alice? A *ghost*? Standing in Darkling's lounge? How could this be real?!

I let my hands fall and looked again. She was still there, swirling near the fireplace.

'Seeing as you found my old *Compendium of Creeping and Crawling Creatures*, I've added some insects to the game.' She chuckled again, sounding like breaking glass.

'Insects?' Something finally clicked in my brain. 'Wait... A.R.M.... is you?'

'Alice Rose Monday. The insect artiste of Darkling Rectory, indeed.' She narrowed her eyes and then moved closer.

'Listen well, Bella Bright. One is close to heaven, God rest her soul. The second is well-employed in the real world, and the third is touching hell. A soul in torment!' She threw her head back and laughed then, and to my ears it sounded like a strangled scream.

'Let's see how good you are at seeking. I need you to look for them, Bella, so we can play hide and seek all night. Don't fail me.'

Then there was a bright shimmer of ice-light, and she faded away. Right before my eyes. Disappeared, and the fire flames did too. I looked for the piano, but it had vanished, and the grey cast to the room gradually lifted and softened, and the colour came back. The headache and the sick feeling faded and, slowly, I found my chest loosened and I could breathe more easily.

Alice's voice sighed into my ear, making me jump like a scalded cat. 'Time is running out. What are you waiting for?'

I swallowed, flicking my eyes around to check she wasn't next to me again.

'You are the seeker. Play my game.'

19

'Did that just happen?' I asked the room, my voice all thick like I'd been screaming.

'What did she say again?' I jabbered, as the adrenaline made me shake. *It's OK, she's gone,* I told myself. I felt like my mind was spinning in silly circles and time was on fast-forward. I needed to get a grip! Three girls' lives were in danger!

'What did she say?' I tried not to shout, screwing up my eyes in frustration. 'Alice Rose Monday. She said... One is close to heaven?' I searched the room for inspiration. 'Up high? Like heaven? The attics? On the roof? Oh my gosh, the clock tower.'

Great. 'I don't even know if I can get up there,' I mumbled as I headed up the stairs at a run.

How did Alice get anyone up there? For a ghost to be able to move things, she would have to be a poltergeist. How can a little harmless spooky whisper thing change into a... vision in the lounge, and also a poltergeist? I tried to recall every spooky film I'd ever seen and ghostly book I'd ever read. There weren't many of either.

'She's a ghost! She probably floated them up!' I snapped at myself, trying to imagine Alice dragging Lex and the duo around the place and hiding them.

'How did you do it, Alice?' I called, and there was giggling in my ear.

'This is all very new to me,' she whispered. 'But because of Halloween. Because of your little friends. Because of the party and the game of hide and seek. The house is with me. It is fun to play with you. A worthy opponent!'

I chewed the inside of my cheek and saved my breath for stair-running. They were steep and tall, all the way up to the top of the house.

At last, my legs burning from the exercise, I tried to catch my breath as I stood at the doorway of the main attic. I had to pluck up my courage before I leaned forward and prodded it open. It swung smoothly, and I got a glimpse of the full attic. Boarded with rough wood, there were dusty boxes and old suitcases, stacked picture frames and broken furniture. It was all absolutely wreathed in thick cobwebs, and I held my arms tightly at my sides as I started across.

When I looked up, I saw a forest of rot, mould and mildew, like a green and black jigsaw overhead, where the roof had leaked. There was a dripping sound from the evening rain, and more spider webs and bulbous black spiders dotted about, their legs all spindly and tense. As the wind swirled around outside, the webs seemed to vibrate, and I gulped.

'Don't anyone dare drop on my head, alright?' I whispered, ducking low. I glimpsed mummified spider husks hanging closer and closer to my face until one scraped my eyebrow. Eight little legs tucked in tightly and I realised it was busy eating something dead. With a disgusted shudder, I decided to move faster and trotted through the middle where the wood beams crossed over. I bounced from one to the next like a clumsy goat, not risking standing on the thinner attic floor, which looked about as safe as an eggshell. It was a long way down, I remembered, feeling giddy.

A tiny door stood right on the far wall, and when I reached it, I rattled the handle. Locked. The house creaked as a gust of wind hit, and I could've sworn that the whole building moved. It made my head swim, so I took a deep breath and counted to ten.

I touched the lock and saw the key was missing. I could have sworn Mum said to leave them in all of the doors so we wouldn't mix them up or lose them. Had it fallen out? Somewhere in the thick dust? Behind me I could see my footsteps, and a thought crossed my mind.

I got on one knee and looked carefully for any other marks. After a few moments I saw long scuffs, like something or someone had been dragged across the dust. 'Someone *is* up there,' I said. 'I knew it!' I had to get through the door.

I started shuffling through the boxes and pieces of furniture closest to me and rifling through piles of curling brown papers. Before long I was yanking open drawers and examining creepy old things.

There was a framed display case of several huge dead butterflies. Urgh. I tried to imagine it on my bedroom wall and shuddered. Lex would probably like it. Who had caught them and spliced them all onto there? I carefully slid it back into a drawer with my fingertips and moved on.

Next along was an old dressing table and soon I was wrenching open the tiny drawers. There was a large black locket on a chain, and curious, I flipped it open. It was full of grey hair, and even a piece of what looked like crusty old skin. I shrieked, dropping it back into the drawer. Underneath it was a silver and tortoiseshell hair comb with long pointed teeth. I turned it over in my hand and pressed a finger on the teeth. They were pretty solid. Maybe I could use it to jimmy the lock.

I took the comb over to the door and slotted the top tooth into the lock hole. I jiggled and wiggled, but nothing happened. My hands were sweaty so I stepped back and wiped them on my jeans.

I tried for ages, slotting in the top comb tooth, then the bottom, different angles, different depths. Nothing. My frustration building, I cocked my head one way and the other, mumbled, 'Here goes...' and karate-chopped the comb vertically downwards. With a loud twang, the lock clicked open and the small door swung out on its hinge.

'OK!' I gasped. 'That worked...'

I stared at the tower stairwell, which was made of blueish wood, reminding me of an ancient castle we'd once visited in France. The steps were very narrow and twisty, and I wondered how I would fit.

I ended up almost crouching due to the cramped space. There were three little flights of this. I pictured Bob the six-foot tall surveyor and realised why he couldn't climb up here.

'How far up is this clock?' I muttered, crawling up and bumping my chin. It was so dark I couldn't see my hands on the steps as I slowly clambered up. The thick dust felt like silk, and billowed up as I moved, making me sneeze.

Suddenly the stairs opened out into the tower itself, and I knocked on the floor, remembering how Mum had said it was so dangerous. It was all rough wooden boards splattered with bird poo but seemed pretty solid. There were tiny slotted gaps in the outer bricks, and the wind whistled through at me. I shivered and tried to peer out. Around me, I could see through the gaps that the dark sky was curdled with grey clouds.

A metre or so above me, the inside of the old clock face gleamed where the moon shone through it. On top of the tower was a small pyramid-shaped pointed roof, and I could see there were huge cracks in it. I spotted a big bird's nest up there, all woven with twigs and moss.

After a moment, I turned around. There was a clock mechanism behind the face, a trunk beneath that, and nothing else.

Where else was closer to heaven than this? Tentatively I edged forward and pushed the trunk with my toe, but it didn't move. There was obviously something heavy inside.

'Hang on,' I said, squinting harder at the trunk. Surely not. How could it be big enough? The duo were both shorter than me, but could one of them really fit in there? Or Lex?

Just then the trunk shifted suddenly toward me, puffing up dust and making me jerk backwards toward the stair-hole, screaming as I windmilled my arms.

20

I fought to regain my balance, letting out a shaky breath and wiping sweat from my brow as I imagined falling down those cramped stairs. Who would rescue the others if I broke my neck?

I stared at the trunk. I *really* did not want to open it. But I had to! What if one of the girls was locked inside? But then... if it wasn't one of them, what on earth could possibly be in there? Something that I really, really didn't want to see. My head was split into two parts... one determined to step forward and flip the lid up and the other equally determined to back off and forget everything – ghosts and misty pianos, the fact that my friends were all hidden around Darkling.

I fought back panicky tears and the end result was I couldn't move.

I took a few massive breaths and dug my fingernails into my palms, forcing myself to creep one step closer. The trunk was still, as if willing me to sneak right up before bursting open with the world's most terrifying jack-in-the-box.

'Shut up!' I hissed to my imagination, clenching my fists. 'Just open it, OK!' I shook my fingers loose and edged closer.

'One... two... Ohhh, I don't want to!' I wailed, my teeth chattering and my panic spiralling up out of control. A bird above me flapped, making me scream and duck. It flew around madly, crashing into the tower walls. Oh no, no, no, this was like being in a horror film. 'Just get it over with!' I yelled, gritting my teeth.

Screwing up all of my courage, I stepped forward and flung the lid of the trunk open, before rolling clumsily backward again, out of the reach of any lurching arms or teeth. A musty smell escaped, and I coughed. After a long minute I inched closer and looked inside. There lay a pile of old grey blankets, covered with dust.

Then the blankets moved, and I fell over backwards, banging my head on the floor behind me.

Suddenly the roof above rumbled and I ducked down, gazing around at the structure in fright. It really wasn't safe here, and I was very high up in the air. I clenched every muscle in my back as I prepared to plummet all the way to the ground, but everything stilled and even the wind outside calmed. 'OK,' I said to myself. The bird flapped once more and settled back into the nest.

Feeling fractionally braver now the trunk stood open and all was still, I peeped in like it was a particularly nasty exhibit in the insect house at the zoo. Just as I was preparing to reach inside and touch the contents, there was another crazy jerk and the blankets wriggled about, as something... someone... coughed and spluttered and tried to sit up.

'Oh my goodness!' I gulped, clutching my chest. 'Regan!'

She wailed, and as I stared at her I felt terror skitter over my skin with millipede legs.

They weren't blankets at all. She was wrapped in a thick, sticky, grey cocoon. She wriggled and moaned, so I gritted my teeth and tried to help. It was a struggle to pull her out, and in shock I saw she was covered in moths. In a panic I slapped the moths off her, hundreds of black flapping creatures large and small crawling over her arms, and it felt like an endless scream was stuck in my throat. They spread out in a terrible torrent, a disgusting waterfall of heavy bodies and papery wings. Some began to fly around my head in rapid circles, their wings buzzing in my ears. The bigger ones on the cocoon moved more slowly and stepped on top of the tiny ones, which scurried and writhed, tangling wings and long, curling antennae together. I shook them off my own hands as I fought to help her.

They tingled like ice, and I was scared they were biting me. Slowly, the matted cocoon ripped off like rotten silk, and I managed to free her arms one by one. We both worked on her legs, the strange fibrous binding thicker around her knees and ankles. She was kicking and thrashing like a human caterpillar, and the puffs of thick dust kept making me cough and sneeze.

When I finally pulled her out of that terrible trunk and held her, standing, swaying beside me, I saw that her face had changed into something terrifying.

'Oh my...' I said, my eyes wide. 'Your face...'

She looked up at me, the tears running down her cheeks. Her face had assumed the pattern on the body of the black moths, a horrible pattern I recognised. Regan had a death's-head skull shading over her face. 'Death's-head hawk-moths!' I muttered, staring at her, the skull glowing in white over her own skull, the dark shadows behind. She looked like she was wearing an incredibly awful Halloween mask, and the effect chilled my blood.

'Right,' I said, clearing my throat and hastily flicking another moth off her chin. 'We need to get down from here.' My bones and muscles were filled with adrenaline, and I wanted to spring up violently and dive down the stairs, away from these hundreds of black moths, now crawling and flying all around us, up the walls of the clock tower, over my feet and knees, making my skin itch.

'Yes please,' said Regan in a quiet voice that made the hair on the back of my neck stand up. The moths were still dropping off her, flipping and buzzing their wings open and I shuddered, trying to move back out of their way. As they fell, though, I blinked in shock. They were vanishing.

'Look!' I stared wildly around. 'They're disappearing! They aren't real!'

Regan managed to peer down as more and more moths winked out of sight. I watched them, mesmerised, and realised I felt slightly better. Vanishing moths were the best kind of moths.

'Yes,' I said, taking her arm, goggling at the disappearing insects. 'Nothing is real. It's all just a big fake-out. I'll go first, and then, Regan— are you concentrating?' She tore her eyes from the mound of moths and up to meet mine with an obvious effort. 'Good. You follow me down these stairs, but make sure you don't fall on me, OK?' I nodded, trying to pull myself together. 'Creeping insects!' I murmured. Just like the ones drawn in that horrid book. How could Alice have done this to Regan? I felt a flash of anger in my chest. What on earth had she done to Lex and Skylar? A huge shudder started at my shoulders and passed through to my feet.

As we slid down the difficult stairs, I peered back, hoping all of those moths would vanish up there and not flit down into the darkness of the clock tower stairs. I took a deep, steadying breath and could still smell the mustiness of the trunk when it opened. She'd been shut in there for nearly an hour, I calculated as we bumped down step after step, her feet kicking into my shoulders. Cocooned with so many moths, flapping and crawling on her. What a nightmare! I risked a glance back, and saw she looked dazed, like someone who had been in an accident, maybe. At the bottom, I took her cold hand and squeezed it.

We made it into the attic and firmly shut the small tower door behind us. The tortoiseshell comb toppled from the lock and I caught it.

'Thank you,' Regan started muttering over and over. I saw her face was looking more normal – the death's-head skin was fading. It was a spooky effect too, just like the moths. I checked the floor around us anxiously.

'A glass of water!' I said brightly. 'Fancy one?' Regan looked at me with dull eyes. The normal insects dead and alive in the attic eaves seemed much easier to deal with as we scampered past.

I hustled her all the way downstairs and

into the kitchen, where I propelled her onto a kitchen chair. I grabbed a glass and took a breath.

'Your face looks... OK, actually,' I said, gently laying a hand on Regan's cheek. 'Back to non-moth-death-mask.'

I clicked my tongue nervously as I ran the tap, standing over her as she drank some. I was pleased to see some colour come back into her cheeks.

'We need to find the others urgently,' I said.

Regan nodded. 'I'll... help you...' she stuttered.

'If you're sure?' I said, sort of glad to no longer be zipping around by myself, but also worried by her strange appearance and her slow speech. Would she really be OK?

'What happened to you?' I asked.

'Al...ice,' she answered, holding her drink tightly. 'We were all together... and then I wasn't...' Regan was staring into space. 'I heard a voice... and she said "Come with me," and I started to say "No – who are you?" And she laughed in my ear in this silvery whisper and sort of drew me with her.'

'Drew you with her?' I repeated, again astonished that a ghost could be so powerful. A proper poltergeist! Able to move people around, and create weird imaginary disappearing insects and change the look of a face! Did Halloween really make ghosts so much stronger?

Regan finished her water and shook her head. A dark moth flew out of her hair and landed on the counter with a soft clunk, and we stared at it. In the light of the kitchen it seemed to melt away into nothingness like a bad dream at sunrise.

'Regan,' I said, 'are you sure you're...'

'I'm fine.' She shook her head again and took a deep breath. 'Let's find Skylar and Lex. If they're in places as awful as I was, we don't have a second to lose.'

'Right!' I said. 'Now I need to think. What were the other clues Alice gave me?'

21

'Something about being employed?' I tried to remember. 'Well-employed?'

Regan drummed her fingers on her arm. 'So, what does that mean?'

'I don't know!'

She stared at me. 'It's your house... and you know who the girl is, don't you? This Alice. Did she used to live here?'

'Mum researched some of the history of this place,' I said, and beckoned her to follow me into the lounge. Mum's pile of notes and books were on a small table in the corner. 'Let's see if she found anything useful.'

'Did you know she'd do this?'

'No, I didn't know she would do anything like this. I just heard her whisper.'

'On the telephone?'

'And before that. And the front door was bizarre.'

'The front door? Why didn't you tell us? Skylar saw her, didn't she? That girl! She even told Skylar that she controlled the doors now, didn't she! Why didn't you say she was a ghost when we were in that bedroom?'

'I didn't know it was her! Anyway, would you have believed me?' I snapped.

She closed her mouth. 'Probably not.'

'Look, never mind that now, OK?' I shuffled about. 'We have more pressing matters.'

'Yeah. Suppose we do. Like your pet ghost suddenly becoming a lot... more powerful.' Regan shook her head. I blinked at her face because it still looked slightly strange. Older, somehow, with sharper cheekbones.

'She was just a whisper.'

'Just a… she's not a whisper any more! Why did you get her to do this to us?'

'Hold on a minute, Regan. I didn't *get* her to do this! I don't control her! I wasn't even sure she was real, to be honest. I thought I was going a bit mad!'

'This whole thing is mad.' Regan pressed her hands to the sides of her head. 'Just like those…' She gulped. '… moths.'

'It's fine,' I said. 'Honestly.' I watched her step up to the mirror over the fireplace.

'Being in that trunk… I don't know.' She hugged herself. 'I've never, ever been so scared.'

I nodded.

'And your ghost did it.' Regan swung around to face me.

'She's not *my* ghost!' I stood up and yelled. 'And the longer we mess about, the longer Skylar and Lex are in trouble!'

'So get reading.' Regan gestured to Mum's notes. 'I could search the internet… But wait… our phones won't work here?'

174

'The broadband people are coming next week to fix the signal,' I said, shuffling through the papers. 'It's driving Mum and me bonkers. OK. I already knew the house had been built in 1750, as a vicarage.'

'There's something,' said Lex, pointing at stuff Mum had typed. 'Additional chapel?'

'Oh yeah,' I said. 'There are the remains of a tiny chapel in the back garden.'

'Great,' said Regan. 'Just what we need. More ghosts.'

'We need to know about previous owners.' I ran my finger down the text, flipping the page over as Regan joined me to skim it.

'There's the vicar from 1850-ish,' said Regan. 'Wasn't Lex on about him? Here.' She pointed at a name.

'Solomon Monday,' I read. I stared at Regan. 'Alice told me her name was Alice Rose Monday. She was his *daughter*.'

I remembered Lex's research project. 'The

daughter who disappeared...' I whispered. My scalp prickled.

The light changed around us, and I felt a tingle of dread like static electricity all over my skin.

'Oh no!' whispered Regan. 'What's happening now?'

The colour of the room seemed to bleed away as everything went grey, like we were in a black and white movie. The now-familiar smell of smoke tickled my nose and I fought the urge to sneeze. We turned our heads at the same time when a pale-faced figure appeared by the kitchen fire.

'The Reverend Solomon Monday was indeed my father,' said Alice in a soft, sighing voice.

'We were j...just trying to find out...' I stuttered.

'The Reverend Solomon Monday. Owner of this house, and also of the chapel yonder.' She turned to look at the corner of the room and I followed her gaze. A ghostly rocking chair had appeared, and a man was sitting in it.

I gasped in shock.

He was dressed in black clothes, with a white

collar, and he was holding a large pipe. His hands were resting on his knees. I saw that he was weeping, as if his whole aura was tormented by utter sorrow. My heart ached just to see him, and a tear sprang from my own eye in sadness for his suffering. Just as I opened my mouth to ask why, he evaporated like steam. Bewildered, I stared back at Alice.

She pointed a thin arm at the window.

'Church!' gasped Regan, and I followed where she was looking. I felt dizzy when, sure enough, under the moon across the end of the rear lawns we could see a church spire.

'But that's impossible!' I breathed. 'It was all demolished and destroyed!'

'Numerous things are impossible,' Alice sighed. 'Like how I played hide and seek many times with my father, but then I could not find him.'

I froze, my mind trying to understand what she was saying. Wait. Was this why we were finishing the game?

'Why couldn't you find him?' I asked. I heard Regan swallow.

'He hid in increasingly challenging places, to make the game more fun,' whispered Alice. 'He wasn't to know that I went looking for him in the wrong place. The wrongest of places.'

There was a blur as a white mist surrounded her, and she stared out of it at us with huge dark eyes.

'What do you mean?' I whispered.

Alice looked down at her leg, the one that hung at a strange angle. She moved it up and down, watching as if fascinated.

'Anyway,' snapped Alice suddenly, making Regan jump. 'We're in the middle of a game here, and I can see you found the first one.' She looked at Regan, and I gulped. Regan was quiet, her hands gripping together like claws.

'Why did you shut Regan in that awful trunk?' I asked, and Alice moved closer. I could see the chill drifting from her, feel the kiss of ice on my face.

'Because she was part of the game,' she sighed

out at me, her mouth again out of sync with what I could hear. 'And moths were the first creepies I studied in detail. The death's-head hawk-moth is particularly thrilling, I find.'

I blinked rapidly, remembering the hundreds of black, crawling, flitting moths.

'We had them on the bushes by the chapel. Huge green caterpillars. Fascinating things.' She moved closer to Regan, eyeing her face. 'A death's-head mask, indeed.' She giggled.

'The game must be finished on Halloween one way or the other. I get to keep them, or you get to find *everyone*.' She whirled around in a misty spiral. 'You two are more intelligent than I considered you to be. You won't find the others, though!' And she laughed, before shimmering in the grey light and vanishing.

My heart seemed to jump back into action and I managed to breathe again, taking a gulp of air and giving myself hiccups. 'I can't believe any of this!' I said. Regan shook her head.

'Let's hurry up and find the others, OK?' I said. 'I don't want to think of what horrific places they might be in.' I tapped my fingers on my teeth. 'But what did she mean about "well-employed"?'

'Well, her dad was a vicar, wasn't he?' Regan was blinking quickly, her hands fluttering like she didn't know what to do with them. She turned around. 'A choir singer? A cleaner? Flower arranger? A maid... they had candles, didn't they? A candle-maker?'

I stared in the mirror over the fireplace and realised I was standing exactly where Alice had stood. Hurriedly I shifted over, and something in the fireplace caught my eye. It was a sooty mark on the old rug. I tried to think back, but I couldn't recall if it had been there before. I knelt down and reached to touch it, thinking that it looked like a footprint. For a long moment I stared into the fireplace. It was large, and above it, of course, was a chimney.

'One thing kids were employed at during Victorian times was as sweeps,' I said suddenly.

'Sweeps? *Chimney* sweeps?' Regan joined me and stared up into the fireplace. 'How many chimneys are in this place?'

'At least... ten...' I said, picturing the tall twirling brick towers dotted all over the uneven roof of Darkling Manor. My mind raced ahead, imagining Alice shoving someone up into the cold darkness... full of damp soot and a feeling of being wedged...

Regan and I stared at each other in alarm.

22

'We'll start here,' I said, trying to sound confident. I didn't want to go poking around up in dirty, dark chimneys, but the thought of one of the girls being up there was frightening. I fell to my knees on the tiles and stared up the chimney. After a moment peering into nothingness, I raced to the hall and grabbed my old umbrella. Gently, I poked it under the lintel and into the flue, calling, 'Is anyone up there?', feeling faintly ridiculous. There was nothing up there but a lot of soot, which fell down onto my face. I stood up, coughing, and we moved on to the next. Regan tried to rub the soot off my face, but ended up with filthy hands. 'Forget it,' I said, picturing the same thing happening another ten times. The kitchen had a chimney that was boarded up, so I left that one. Regan stayed close to me as I raced about, trying to remember where the chimneys were. The parlour's fireplace was covered in dust sheets, whereas the study had more of an ornamental one, which was tiny. We completed the circuit of the ground floor by noting the dining room and glass house didn't have one.

'Upstairs?' asked Regan, and I nodded. We checked all of the first floor's six bedrooms, treading very carefully on the right-hand side of the stairs. No bedroom fireplaces had any rogue chimney sweeps.

'Are you sure this idea is right?' Regan asked, just as I was thinking the exact thing. I shrugged.

'I don't have anything better?'

'Would kids have been employed in the house in other ways? Like... as scullery maids?' asked Regan.

I nodded. And gardening helpers, probably a coal boy... 'Darn it! The clue is too hard.'

'Let's keep checking all of the chimneys,' she said, as I looked at my watch and felt sick at the thought of Mum coming home in three hours. How would I explain I'd 'lost' two of the guests? With the lack of any other good ideas we continued up to the second floor. The three huge suites had enormous fireplaces and chimneys, but the prodding umbrella revealed all were empty.

'That's it,' I said. 'Total chimney count fourteen, I think.'

'Did any of them seem different?' asked Regan, and I stuck out my bottom lip.

'Nope,' I said after a moment. 'All empty, all normal, except for the kitchen's chimney, which was boarded up.'

'What's behind the boards?' we asked in unison, and we stared at each other.

'Oh no! Alice wouldn't have *boarded* her up in a chimney, surely?' I lost my breath as we started to run down the stairs, pelting along the hall and sliding into the kitchen.

Once there we froze, and I clutched Regan. 'Listen!' I whispered, and we stood still, listening to the house.

There was silence for a long moment, aside from the howling wind.

I tiptoed across the kitchen to move my ear closer to the chimney. There was a tiny clicking.

'I heard something!' I frantically mouthed.

Regan frowned and tiptoed closer too. After a long moment I saw her eyes widen and knew that she had heard it too.

'Is that... *scratching*?' I said, staring in horror at the chimney. It seemed so small!

'We need something to get those boards off,' said Regan, already pulling at the nails that had been hammered into the old wooden surround. 'How about a knife? Or a fork?'

I shook my head. 'We're not eating dinner here!' Moving to a cupboard, I pulled out Mum's massive toolbox. 'Now we're talking.' I rubbed coal dust out of my eyes and flipped the lid.

A huge array of tools gleamed dully in the kitchen light.

I ticked over them with my fingers and pulled out two large flat-head screwdrivers. 'These'll work,' I said, passing her one and showing her how to wrench the boards out. 'They're only light plywood.'

We started levering with the screwdrivers, and carefully pulled out the top board. Behind it was a slice of utter darkness.

'Hello?' I whispered into the void. We leaned forwards, straining to see anything when there was a loud whimper, and suddenly a blue eye popped open in the gap. I jumped, screaming out in shock. Regan reeled backwards, arms waving until she lost her balance. I ducked to avoid the screwdriver she bowled up into the air.

'Oh my God!' I yelled. 'Eye! There is someone in there!'

'It's Skylar!' said Regan. I stared at her, shocked by how pale she had gone.

'Are you alright?'

'Yes! We have to hurry, though. We have to save her...'

We snatched up the screwdrivers again and levered under the lower pieces of wood. They snapped off, sending nails tinkling on the kitchen tiles and opening the tiny gap of the fireplace into something bigger and darker.

Skylar had obviously been fighting to escape, as soot was puffing like an old-fashioned train. I coughed as it tickled my throat and stung my eyes.

'Can you get out?' I called up there, wondering how she had even fitted into that chimney. Then something fell out and clicked onto the fireplace tiles, and wriggled around, tiny legs waving in the air.

'What is *that*?!' shrieked Regan. I stared down at the thing, and realised it was a speckled beetle. I held my breath. A deathwatch beetle.

Skylar was kicking, scrabbling around more

inside the chimney, and sooty dust was billowing everywhere.

Another beetle plopped out and clicked around on the tiles, bashing into the first one like a mini dodgem car. I stared at them, thinking about the beetle illustrations in the creeping and crawling book.

'Help me!' came a thin cry, and I tore my eyes from the beetles and up to the fireplace, trying not to scream. The soot burned my throat, and I let out a strangled cough.

The eye was there again, and the open chimney now revealed more of Skylar's face. I realised in horror how filthy she was. She looked like a ghost herself, a waif-like little chimney sweep, black-streaked and miserable. Then I frowned. There was something wrong with her face too... like the death's-head had looked on Regan. Skylar's skin was oddly shiny... just like a beetle shell. I squinted. With the classic golden speckle too. I stared at her in amazement, her skin gleaming and glittering beneath the fine layer of soot. Another beetle dropped from her, and I realised the chimney was full of them, wriggling and clicking their little legs.

And Skylar was wedged in there with them.

Upside down.

'Grab her arms!' I yelled at Regan. She scrabbled around with me, our hands in the chimney space, and instantly looked puzzled.

'I can't reach them!'

'So just grip what you can!' I felt like I was on fast-forward, moving too quickly to think properly, my mind not wanting to concentrate on poor Skylar boarded up in a chimney, beetles crawling all over her. Nope. NOPE.

'Grab what I can?' Regan was shouting. 'She's wedged! Like a cork in a bottle! I can only reach her head!'

'So get hold of it!'

We both got our hands around Skylar's head,

and tried to pull her down. She moaned pitifully.

'Oh my gosh, why does it feel strange... on her hair... like feathery...?'

'What?' I spluttered, leaning as close as I could and examining the top of Skylar's head. Regan was right: there were two strange little antennae growing.

'It's OK,' I tried to soothe her. Regan was crying. 'It's just a creepy effect thing...' I hoped, anyway.

She's stuck in there!' Regan's tears were making her soot-streaked face even more filthy.

'What about... I don't know... butter? Water?'

'Butter?' Regan glared at me like I'd gone mad.

'Yeah, like I don't know... grease her up?' I didn't want to admit I'd been gazing around the kitchen for inspiration. I stared at Skylar's face, thinking as hard as I could. 'Can you move your legs?'

She moaned again, and then I saw her eyes close and there was a shuffle, and a pile of soot fell out from around her onto the fireplace.

'Aha!' I yelled. 'Your legs are free, right?'

'Yes,' she moaned. 'It's my arms – my arms hurt. They're all tangled around me.'

I had a flash of horror that she'd have six arms now... just like a deathwatch beetle, and clamped my teeth together to stop my rising panic.

'OK, don't worry. You'll be alright, we'll get you out,' I gabbled again. How could Alice have done this? She would have needed massive strength to flip Skylar upside down and shove her into a chimney.

'We need to call the fire brigade!' shouted Regan, who was pacing up and down. The beetles were bombing around the fireplace in circles, trapped by the raised edges of brick. Their tiny feet were clicking on the surface, and I glanced down at their sturdy little bodies, shuddering.

I grabbed hold of her and put my hands on her shoulders. 'She'll be alright, Regan, I promise. We'll get her out; we'll figure it out.'

She took a giant shaky breath. 'I don't like this game.'

'Nor me,' coughed a little voice from inside the chimney.

'Can you free your arms?' I tried. 'Just bit by bit? Imagine you're working on a knot in your shoelaces or something? Slowly work them loose?'

'I've been trying,' said Skylar. 'There are so many beetles up here, I can't tell you... it's awful...'

'I know,' I said. 'But they're only beetles. They're OK. It'll be alright, Skylar.'

'Just get me out!' Her voice turned into a high scream, and I winced.

There was a rustle and a bump, and several more beetles fell out.

'Gross!' said Regan, screwing her face up like an old woman.

'There's more space now,' gasped Skylar. 'I can move one arm... hang on...'

We waited for long moments, as more rustles and scrapes came from the chimney.

'The more soot and... things that come out,'

I said, 'the more room you'll have to shift around a bit.'

'Things,' repeated Regan, doing an elaborate body shudder. The beetles in the fireplace were all clambering over each other now, making little beetle pyramids and falling over.

'I'm going to kick myself... down,' said Skylar, spluttering as a beetle partly went into her mouth. 'Yuck YUCKY!' she said, spitting violently. I heard her screaming through her closed lips, and then some quiet thuds. She slithered down a few centimetres.

'Yes!' I yelled. 'You can do it, Skylar! Come on!'

She grimaced. We could see her whole head and some of her neck now. It was filthy with soot. The little antennae on top of her head wriggled. Regan and I stared at them, and then at each other.

'We have to get her out of there faster,' said Regan.

I stared around the kitchen and thought about Regan's earlier suggestions of knives and forks.

Maybe she wasn't too far away from a good idea, I thought, as I ran to the utensil drawer and started rattling through Mum's cooking bits and bobs. A lemon juicer? No. A potato masher? No.

Rolling pin... ladle... Then I saw a palette knife and I grabbed it. And a fish slice, solid metal with a flat head for flipping fish in the pan.

'Here!' I shouted, tossing the flat-edged palette knife to Regan. 'Get that up the sides of the chimney and see if you can't knock some more beet... I mean things... out.'

'Oh my God. I literally can't believe I'm going to do this,' said Regan. 'I *hate* beetles so much. Crunchy little devils.'

'Crunchy?' I said. 'That's vile.' I prayed that they'd be like the moths and disappear when we rescued Skylar.

Regan and I worked feverishly around Skylar, me shoving the fish slice up the inner bricks of the chimney on the right, Regan on the left. It was sort of like stripping wallpaper, I thought, as soot and beetles tumbled down. I tried to ignore them sliding over my hand but had to bite hard on my tongue and shake like crazy when one went up my sleeve. Regan was the same, jabbing the fish slice up and down, jerking back in horror when the beetles got too close.

Despite the chilly kitchen I was boiling hot, the sweat making my forehead damp. Soot ran down my face and burned my eyes. I could taste it, like ashy cindery tar. My arm muscles and my neck ached, so I switched hands.

After six or seven minutes and the occasional 'Ouch!' from Skylar, there was a rumble inside the chimney.

'She's falling!' yelled Regan, and we dropped the scrapers and held out our hands.

'Mind the beetles,' said Regan, as Skylar jerked downwards and bumped her head on the fireplace tiles, her legs still up the chimney.

'OY!' she shouted. 'Never mind the beetles. Weren't you supposed to catch me?'

196

'Sorry,' I said, doing my best to yank her outwards.

'Why do I feel like the world's weirdest midwife?' asked Regan, and I couldn't help but smile. It was exactly like we were delivering a baby from the chimney, pulling Skylar out of the hole.

'It's a girl!' I snorted ridiculously.

Skylar screamed as her legs finally tumbled out, rolling us all over until my head banged into the table leg. Regan had managed to duck out of the way and was peering at us quizzically. 'Everyone alright?' she asked, and I smiled, thinking she sounded almost normal.

Then I saw that she was staring at the beetles and, slowly, they started to disappear. 'Just like the moths,' she breathed, and I crawled back across to watch.

'I think we'd better make Skylar a quick drink too, maybe a cup of tea,' said Regan, as we helped her stand up and brushed soot from her arms. ' Plus we all need a shower.'

I patted the soot from her head, and puffed out a relieved breath when I realised the antennae were shrinking.

As we watched the wriggling stick-like appendages vanish, I hated to think what might have happened if Skylar had been stuck longer... would she have really grown six arms?

Skylar pressed fingers to her skull. 'I have a headache from being upside down for so long,' she complained. 'In all of my life, I have never—'

'Just sit still a while,' I interrupted her. 'You'll feel better, I'm sure.'

'It's the light,' she said. 'After the chimney, everything seems too bright. It hurts. Even Regan's face looks wrong.'

'Not as wrong as it was,' I said. Regan rolled her eyes and I nodded to myself. They seemed OK.

'I'm not turning the lights off,' I said. I knew the beetles were disappearing, but I still didn't like the idea of them clicking around the kitchen in the dark. Poor Skylar. I glanced at Regan, who was pressing her fingertips into her cheekbones. Skylar shuffled stiffly to the window and stared out. Her sooty feet crackled on the kitchen's tiled floor, and I wondered if I'd get time to mop it before Mum got home. Unlikely. The moon shone in at us, and I heard Skylar take deep breaths as I boiled the kettle.

She coughed. 'We need to get out of here!'

I stirred lots of sugar into the tea. Bad for teeth, yes, but good for shock. Apparently. I was acutely aware we still had to find Lex, and I was getting worried about how long it was taking to find everyone. I checked my watch again and saw it was nearly ten o'clock.

Skylar ran hot water in the sink and washed her arms and her face over and over. After a bit I joined her, quickly washing my own face and hands as best as I could. Our clothes were ruined, all soot-streaked and smeared as badly as if we'd rolled around on the remains of a bonfire. The kitchen stank of soot, and now there were puddles of water mixing with the dust, making the floor slippery. The chimney boards were scattered around, alongside the sooty kitchen implements. No time to worry about any of it, though, as I pictured Lex in my mind. I knew that wherever she was, she really needed our help – and fast.

Skylar kept coughing, the soot obviously irritating her throat. I made her gulp down the tea and then we all gathered to discuss the final clue. The words lit up in my head like the afterburn of a lightning flash.

'The third touching hell and close to torment.'

'Just Lex left to find,' I said. 'We can do it. We're winning!' I patted Regan's shoulder gently as everything went grey.

'Oh no! It's Alice again!' I whispered, the familiar dread bubbling like acid in my stomach. She appeared as if she was approaching through thick fog. Suddenly she seemed very close indeed. Her damaged leg swung to the side, making her limp with a jerking stagger.

'Well, well, well,' she said, and I studied her face. She seemed bigger and was now much taller than us. I had the idea that in some ways she was younger, but in others she seemed to be older than Mum. I could perceive more detail of her face, dark eyes deep-set beneath strong eyebrows. Her plaits swung as she limped, and again I wondered why they seemed damp.

The duo and I shrank together and backed off, for she was big. And clearly angry.

'So you found another?' She raised heavy eyebrows, her face solemn and her mouth thin and twisted on one side. 'I hope I didn't make the game too easy for you?'

'Y...y...yes, I mean no!' I said, trying to be brave. Unfortunately, my voice trembled like a tiny baby. 'It was difficult enough, thank you.'

'Good, because the game has to be played right. It can't be too easy for you to win. It must be a challenge.' She stared at me. 'It looks like I will only have one playmate for the next hundred and seventy years.' She laughed, an odd harsh sound that reminded me of a crow. 'I will keep her and play hide and seek with her here forever. Unless you can seek her out, of course. Are you able to finish the game, I wonder?'

I stiffened. 'Weren't you meant to be a vicar's daughter?'

'Yes, indeed I am! My father is the leader of the church here at Castleton, and a respected pillar of the community!' She was shouting now, her eyes burning with dark fire. Little flecks of white spit shot out of her mouth, and some caught in her hair.

'Why are you so angry?' I said, and she swirled closer to me. Her figure was surrounded by shimmering silvery tendrils, which flowed when she moved.

My brain was trying very hard not to be utterly terrified at the sight of this ghost, this awful girl who played such terrible games, but still some small part of me wondered *why*. What had happened to her?

She laughed, and it sounded like all the coldest winds of winter. The sound made me picture animals trapped in the ice, their hearts freezing. I shivered.

I risked a look away from her to Regan and

Skylar, who were in each other's arms, shaking.

'I've been...different... well, *dead*; in this house ever since that Halloween, 1863.' She swirled in a spiral, and I couldn't help but raise my hands to protect my face as she loomed over us for a moment. 'Pa died in spring 1888, I think. Time is blurry. He's gone, but the unfinished game keeps me here. I just long to play. When you came to Darkling, Bella, I watched all the time. The very first girl to live in the house since myself. You had a *mother.*' She was silent for a long moment, and I hardly dared breathe.

'My mother died after she gave birth to me,' she said. 'November 13th 1851. A birthday, a death-day.'

'I'm sorry,' I whispered.

'I watched your mother, and how she loved you. I began to understand what I had lost. I never knew her! The angel Lillian, Pa called her. You have everything, Bella. Everything I do not. All I have is this cursed darkness, all alone. I'm so tired of it!'

Tears sprang to my eyes at the thought of Mum, and I bit my lip to stop myself from crying.

She stared at the floor for a long moment, and nobody dared move.

'Other families had been here, of course, but beside one disgusting boy, none had children. I watched you and began to see myself in you. You were just as I was, quiet and lonely. I imagined us as a coin, me on one side, and you on the other. You even look like me!' I saw Skylar and Regan stare from me to her. I didn't, did I?

She reached out a white hand to me, and I gaped at it. No way was I holding her *hand*. I swallowed.

'But then... tonight... is my one chance to finish the game.' For a moment she seemed to shrink, her shoulders dropping. 'I couldn't find my father, my pa, but maybe you will be able to find your friend, and win the game.'

My own eyes filled with tears because something about the tone of her voice was heart-breaking. I tried to imagine a hundred and seventy years all alone, and, despite everything she had done, for a second I almost wanted to hug her.

'I just wanted someone to spend the years with.' She put her hands behind her back and limped away from us, closer to the fireplace. 'Sometimes I know I must find a way to move on, to break free and follow Pa, but I am scared. I know every inch of this house, my beloved rectory. I watch my creepies and I never want to leave. But at other times, I have begun to feel a longing, and I dream of seeing my father, even my mother...' Everything was still grey around her, but her steps were heavy, as though there was real weight behind them. How was she so real? I realised I was trembling.

I thought of Lex to make me brave. 'Maybe you could see your p...pa again, and your ma. We can help... we can finish things for you. But please, Alice? What have you done with Lex?' I said, and Alice turned slowly back to me.

'I know *she* is the one you consider your truest friend,' she said, and I felt my mouth stretch downwards in dismay. 'She had to be the one I've sent to hell.'

I looked wildly at Regan and Skylar and they gazed back at me, their mouths dark circles of horror. I clasped my hands to my head in frustration and fear.

'Where is she?!' I screamed. 'You won't have her! You can't keep her!'

'Yes!' yelled Regan. 'We'll find her!'

'Maybe,' Alice said, and, shaking her head at us, she wrapped herself into a silver mist, slowly disappearing. 'Maybe not. This will be very difficult. Even impossible. Perhaps I will have one playmate or even two if someone... falls. Oh yes... I've made the insects bigger this time...' I took a step back as the mist spread, not wanting it to touch me.

'Oh no,' I said, feeling like I wanted to cry.

'She's a monster.' Skylar's voice was sharp. 'We have to get rid of her, right? Get her out of here forever.'

I nodded. 'But how?'

'The game,' Regan said. 'She told us! Her hide and seek game is still going on.'

'Yes,' I said. 'She never found her father, remember? So she went somewhere *wrong*? The *wrongest* place?'

'So that's it,' said Regan, a grim look on her face.

I nodded. 'We have to find Lex as soon as we can. But to finish the game I think we also have to find Alice.'

'Alice said Lex is in hell,' I said, my forehead furrowed with fear. I tried not to think about *bigger* insects.

'Mmm.' Regan screwed up her face. 'Somewhere you don't want to fall. Hell is hot, right?'

'Yep.'

'So where in this house is hot?'

'I don't know. Erm... the boiler?' I tried to think.

'Alice wouldn't actually... like... *boil* Lex, would she?' Regan looked aghast.

I ran for the stairs. 'It's in a cupboard in the room with the bath on the first floor. Come on!'

'Room with the bath? Don't you mean the bathroom?' asked Skylar.

'It's just a room with a bath in it, nothing else at all,' I puffed. 'Mum and I just called it "the room with the bath" so we knew which room we meant.'

We ran as fast as we could, and I tripped on the top step and managed to bash my chin on the wall.

'Ouch.' I rubbed it as everyone swung left and followed the passageway to the room with the bath, a once-white tiled room with a huge bath that actually had feet. The tiles were cracked and filthy, but the room had promise. I remember Mum crowing when she saw it. 'An absolute gem!' she'd called it. Personally I thought the toes on the feet were a little too monsterish for my liking. *Mum*, I thought suddenly. Currently on a train, racing towards us.

We slammed through the door like rugby players and then I had to squeeze around Regan to get to the boiler cupboard. It had been one of the first things Mum had checked, as she wouldn't risk us here with no heating over the winter.

I was glad, because if it had been summer she wouldn't have bothered. Having hot water was an awesome luxury in our business.

I flipped open the mouldy door and eyed the old thing, a huge copper lozenge surrounded by complicated pipes. Regan bent over and peered into the darkness at the back, but there was no sign of Lex.

'Where else is hot?' she asked as I shut the door and stared at her, trying to think.

'It's not really a hot house, generally,' I said, and then frowned. The glass house was a sort of hot house in the warm months, and maybe it could be a type of hell. Lex had hidden there earlier; could she be there again?

'Let's try the glass house!' I said, and we ran back downstairs again. We skidded on past the kitchen on the right, and instead went left into the formal dining room. It was all panelled in dark wood and had dead stuffed animals dotted around. They stank of something close to cat wee.

212

I wrinkled my nose and charged down the room to reach the stained-glass doors for the glass house.

Inside, shadows waved and changed even though all was calm outside now the rain had stopped. I blew out a steadying breath and went in, holding a hand up to my nose as if to protect it from the smell of damp rot and mouldy soil. I remembered the creeping vines and dead insects and picked up my feet. I didn't want anything winding around my ankles in the dark.

'What are you guys going to grow in here?' asked Skylar, wide-eyed.

'Potted palms, Mum mentioned. And cacti. I like those Venus flytraps, those ones that eat insects,' I said, my voice funny from holding my nose.

'There's just some sort of vine wrapping itself around everything at the moment,' she said, kicking part of it with her foot.

There was a rustling sound and I sprang back like a cat who'd seen a cucumber. Had it moved?

'She's not in here so let's go, OK?' gabbled Regan, and Skylar and I nodded vigorously. We whirled out, and I shut the door firmly behind us. Didn't want that vine getting into the main house, I thought, even though that was a mad idea, surely. I took a deep breath and pulled my plait over my shoulder. Alice and the general creepiness of the house was obviously affecting me. What a Halloween this was shaping up to be! To think I'd been worried the party would be boring!

I laughed to myself but it turned into a sob. I just wanted to find Lex now.

'What's funny?' asked Skylar.

'Turned out to be an interesting party after all!' I said. 'You told me to make sure you didn't have a dull time.'

'I think we may have got more than we bargained for,' said Regan, shaking her head slowly. 'So there's nowhere else hot?'

'Just think a minute. One in heaven, one well-employed,' I said, pointing at Regan and Skylar in turn. 'Wait,' I said, suddenly. 'Are we stupid or what?'

'What?' Regan blinked.

'If heaven is up high, then hell must be...' I opened my eyes wide and nodded at her.

'Down low?'

'Yep.'

Together we moved down the hall back to the front door, and then along to the best parlour, where the other door was located.

'Oh my God,' Regan said. 'Are you sure about this?'

I put my hand on the door handle. 'No.'

With a twist of my wrist, the black door opened, and we stared down into the darkness.

The cellar.

26

'We do this together,' hissed Regan, as we took a first step down into hell.

'Agreed,' I said, even though I'd gone very sweaty. I puffed air like I was blowing up balloons and we descended a few more steps, still bathed in the light from above. We'd gripped hands, and I found myself in the middle. A rose between two thorns, I thought, madly. They were no longer the deadly duo... instead we were the terrified trio... I felt like I was going to be sick.

I was trying to squint at what was below us when there was a loud bang, and we were plunged into utter darkness. Everything was still, and then Regan screamed in my ear.

'What's happening?!'

'The door's closed!' I yelled back. 'It's OK!'

'I don't like it!' yelled Skylar.

'Nor me!' I yelled back. 'We should have brought a torch!'

'Why didn't you think of that!'

'I don't know! Sorry, OK? Why didn't *you* think of it?'

'It's not my house!'

'It's not really my house either!' I yelled.

'Darkling is more your house than our house!'

'Just shush, OK! I'm trying to think!'

'I don't know what's down there and it's freaking me out!' Regan's voice was getting a bit hoarse with all the shouting.

'I've never been down here before either!' I said. 'Have you got anything that we can use to light up where we are? I don't want to turn around on the step together because I'm worried we might fall.'

'Fall?!' Regan yelled again. 'We can't *fall*!'

'No, I definitely don't want us to fall.' I squeezed her arm. 'It's OK, right? We can do it.'

'I have my phone!' Skylar shouted suddenly.

'It won't work, though – we can't call for help; we already know this,' I said, shaking my head in the dark.

'Don't shake your head at me,' she snapped, elbowing me in the ribs. 'I can feel you doing it!'

'Sorry,' I mumbled.

'What I mean is, Bella, my phone has a super-bright light!' With a click we could suddenly see again, and I grinned at her.

'My phone has all the gadgets,' she said smugly.

'So does mine!' said Regan, fumbling in her pocket. 'But it's run out of battery.'

'Ah well, mine has a guaranteed battery life—' Skylar showed us her phone. 'Right here, see...'

'OK, OK! Brilliant. Now don't point it in my eyes!' I fended her off. 'It's bright!'

She shone it down the steps, and I gulped. 'Down?' she asked.

'Might as well,' I said. 'Even though I never wanted to do anything less in my life.'

Regan squeezed my hand.

We took careful steps down, and as we got lower I wondered when we'd reach the bottom.

'How deep is it?' asked Skylar wonderingly, sounding a little braver now because she had the light.

'Very.' I paused. 'What can I hear?'

We froze, and Skylar played the light below us. 'Dripping water?' she said.

'Oh yeah!' I thought about Mum's notes. 'Back in the day, this place had its own water supply! Fascinating, apparently, and very unusual. A well.'

'Well what?' said Regan.

'No, *a* well,' I said again.

'I knew your water tasted dirty,' said Skylar.

'We don't actually drink the stuff from down here,' I said. 'It's all dried up now.'

'Tell me, please. Tell me that we're not going to find Lex down the bottom of some well?'

Regan's voice got higher and more worried-sounding.

I opened my mouth to reply but nothing came out.

Without speaking we kept on down the stairs, which were wooden and becoming more warped and slippery the lower we stepped. There was damp in the air, a stench of dirty water and pondweed. It was underlined by another smell, even worse. Sharp, like farmyard waste. The dripping sped up, and I noticed it had grown cold.

Our feet finally hit the stones of the cellar floor and we clung on to each other's arms. Skylar swept the tiny phone torch around the cellar. It was big, and there were piles of boxes and old ropes in the corners. The roof was dark and uneven and curved down at the edges, giving the feeling of being inside an eerie cave.

I could hear the other two gasping, gurgling water and a skittering, scurrying sound.

'What *is* that?' whispered Regan sharply.

Something white ran past, but Skylar couldn't move her light fast enough to see what it was. I started to get a very bad feeling.

Only one of Alice's compendium 'creepies' ran like that. From the last page I'd seen.

Spiders.

My skin shivered at the thought of giant white spiders scurrying around us, and I clenched my teeth to get a grip of myself. Panic was making me want to tear upstairs like a mad thing and lock the cellar door forever, never to come down here again. It seemed to feel less like a cellar and more like a dungeon with every second that passed.

'Where is the well?' asked Regan, and I stared around.

'Hold the light... Over there... no... there!' I said as Skylar whipped it around too fast, leaving us with nothing but a blurred afterglow. More white things ran around, getting closer to our feet.

'What is that?' said Regan, her voice shaking.

'No well here,' Skylar said. We moved forward a couple of steps.

'Careful, as it might not have a... **WOAH!!!**' I screamed. We teetered on the edge of a sudden, gigantic hole in the floor, and only managed to not fall in by throwing ourselves backwards. I was pretty sure I was having a heart attack, and Regan was scream-weeping.

'Oh no! Oh no! We could've fallen in!' she was blathering. I groped for her hands in the darkness and squeezed them.

'We're OK! Regan, listen to me! We're OK!'

Skylar was lying flat on her back, breathing raggedly in and out, and I noticed it was pitch black.

'Skylar! Turn on the light!' I said.

I heard a strangled sob. 'I can't! I dropped it!' After a second of cursing her in my head, I gripped for her hand too. Long moments passed before she calmed down, but then something with lots of tiny sharp feet ran over my ankle. Quietly I drew my foot up under me because I didn't want anything else like that *ever* touching me again. My brain was screaming SPIDER! But I sucked in my cheeks and somehow kept it inside, not wanting to freak the other two out any more.

'We have to look down there,' I said eventually. 'If you can't, then I will – just give me a moment.'

I started to think in detail of the giant torch Mum had upstairs somewhere, especially for old dark houses with questionable electrics. 'Idiot,' I cursed myself over and over. Why hadn't I grabbed it as we headed to the cellar door!

Although then we'd actually *see* the spiders... and I really didn't want to. Why did Alice even like insects so much? Although spiders weren't actually insects, my brain gabbled, they were arachnids.

'Shut up!' I growled at myself, as I wriggled onto my front and held out my hands in front of me. Where was the edge of the well? I felt the slick stone carefully with my fingers and found it less than a metre away. The thought of us all falling down there made my head spin in horror.

How could anyone build a whole well without a surrounding wall for safety? I shook my head at the danger and the stupidity at play here, and inched forwards so that I could look down.

The well was huge and deep, but immediately I saw something odd. There was a tiny light at the bottom. 'Skylar!' I hissed. 'Your phone! I can see the light!' I had to lean further in to better see and let my arms fall down inside to support my neck. 'Lie on my legs, Skylar,' I said, and felt slightly better when her weight added to my own to give me extra security. The thought of sliding forward and falling in head first was hideous.

I leaned and breathed in the putrid stink of a hundred and seventy-odd years of wet rot.

'Oh God, this is vile to the power of a million,' I said, my voice echoing in the well.

'Who's there?' came a tiny high voice from below me, and I gasped, jerking like a puppet and nearly bouncing Skylar off my feet.

'What?' I managed to say, and I felt Regan lean over next to me. 'Lex... is that you?'

'Is that really her?' Regan murmured, gripping the edge of the well.

'Careful,' I said, and she moved back slightly. 'Lie on both our legs, right, Skylar?'

I had to get my head lower. My knees were being painfully squashed into the stone floor by Skylar's weight. The well was dripping all around me, and the light down there moved.

A small, pale face, looking up. A pair of tiny glasses, glinting and reflecting.

'Lex?' I screamed.

'I'm down here,' said the voice, and my mind

went into super slow-motion. 'Guys! I see you! Your faces are dark but I see you! Talk to me! Stay with me!'

'Lex! We found you! We're here, it's OK!' I gabbled. Only then I realised how cold it was in the well. I cast my hand about a little and realised it was freezing, like a tomb. The walls were dank, with ice-cold moisture dribbling down like the well stones were weeping. Then I squinted at them and realised the walls were *moving*.

Something, or a thousand white somethings... were crawling on the walls of the well.

'Is my phone OK?' called Skylar. I shoved her with my foot.

'Oof! I just wanted to know!' she sounded sulky.

I shook my head, feeling like I couldn't think quickly enough. I yelled as loudly as I could. 'Lex! Are you OK? Did Alice throw you down there?' Surely she was lucky to be alive after a fall like that.

'She didn't throw me,' called up Lex. 'It was

weird, like I floated down. But I'm not OK! I'm freaking out... it's really cold. I don't like it down here! The phone light is better but it hit my ankle, though, and that hurt...'

I squinted down at her and realised she looked different somehow... her hair. Her hair had turned white. I thought about Regan's death's-head mask, and Skylar's antennae and beetle-skin. The white hair made her look old, even ghostly. I didn't like it. I reminded myself that those other effects had disappeared... so hopefully Lex's hair would go back to her trademark bright ginger colour again.

There was a pause as we heard her sob and I guessed everyone was trying to wrap their heads around this nightmare.

'You're going to get me out, right?' screamed Lex. 'Don't you leave me here, please. Thanks for the phone light, though. Did I say that? It's so nice to have light. It means I can see *them*.'

She let out a large whimper, which echoed and sounded like ten people were weeping.

'Lex!' I called, reaching down to her with an outstretched hand. 'Don't be upset! We'll get you out.'

'Them?' murmured Regan in my ear. 'What...' Then I realised she must have noticed the well walls.

'Oh. My. God...' she said. SPIDERS EVERYWHERE!!'

28

'How are we going to... wait! What's in the boxes over there?' I said, as Skylar, Regan and I slid ourselves back from the well edge and slithered across the wet stones with care. One slip, I realised, and anybody could die down here. *Alice!* I thought. How could she have done this?! We moved on cautiously. The dripping rang in my ears, and one freezing drop splatted the middle of my head making me jerk forwards.

A thought occurred to me. Alice wouldn't have come looking down *here* for her father, all those years ago, in her last game of hide and seek... would she? Could this have been the *'wrongest'* place? With effort, I pushed her out of my head and started feeling around in the boxes, waiting for my eyes to adjust to the gloom.

I started off being scared about what I was touching, but the image of Lex down in the well was burned into my brain forever and it made me want to move fast and less cautiously. I felt wooden crates with wet packing paper inside, a rickety ladder, some old ropes, and a box of wet candles. And more spiders. My fingers accidentally brushed the back of one, and I felt its muscles bunch as it flexed around to try and bite me. My shoulders clenched as I fought to hold in a scream. I could see the movement now, the glimmer of hundreds of tiny black eyes. They were white. Big. Hairy. And had eight legs. They were streaming in and out of holes in the cellar walls. Oblong bodies, I thought, white appearance. Alice's creeping creatures book had described them. Ghost spiders.

I tried to think of the vanishing death's-head hawk-moths and deathwatch beetles and tell myself they weren't real, but the creeping clicking made my skin shrink, and I swiped at them with the backs of my wrists. Even though my eyes had got more used to the darkness, it was difficult to see in the gloom.

'Ugh, what was that? Disgusting,' said Skylar, feeling around with her hands. 'I flipping felt the massive legs on one, even stroked it, for goodness' sake.'

'Erm, Skylar,' I said. 'We have to remember that they are just an illusion and they *will* disappear when we find Lex. They really *will*.'

'What are you rabbiting on about, Bella?' snapped Skylar. 'Another one just walked over my leg.' She gulped. 'I can do this. But, I really, really, really *hate* spiders.'

'Girls!' I said in a firm voice. 'They aren't real, and we have to concentrate on Lex now, OK, so—'

'One is sitting on my hand!' scream-whispered

Skylar. She flung her hand about like she was possessed. 'It was heavy! They are tarantula-size! Why are they so big? I thought it was going to bite me!' I felt her shudder and flap both hands round in panic.

'This is useless,' I muttered.

'Ouch! My head! Look at that,' said Regan, after shuffling further around the well edge and bumping her shoulder on a huge metal hook that clanked on the ceiling. 'What would that be for?'

I groped about and followed her voice. 'Meat? Other equipment? The well *bucket*?' I said, as I reached out for it and felt the clammy metal. The wheels in my mind started turning. 'Guys! That's what we have to do! Use the hook to tie the ropes, and we can throw them down. Then Lex can climb out.'

There was silence as the duo considered the idea.

'All the way up that well?' said Regan doubtfully. 'By herself?'

'We have to try!'

We gathered all of the ropes we could find and

I dragged the ladder across. We sat cross-legged and started knotting them together. There were sixteen, all different thicknesses. I tried not to worry about the thin ones. Or the spiders inside the well. The darkness mellowed to a gloom as my eyes became accustomed to the lack of light.

'Will they be long enough?' asked Skylar, cursing when she knotted her fingers into the loops.

It seemed to take ages, and I was worried about how cold the well was. Lex had been down there for so long. I couldn't see my watch down here, but I knew midnight was creeping closer. If Mum knew what we were doing down here, I would be in so much trouble. I took a deep breath and shook the worries out of my head. I needed to focus on one thing. Saving Lex.

When we were done and all three of us had yanked on the knots to make sure they held, I tossed one rope end up to the hook. The darkness and the fact that the rope was so wet and heavy meant it took several goes to get it securely over.

We let out a ragged cheer when at last I managed, my wrist and elbow aching.

Regan grabbed it and swung on it for a moment to test what weight it would carry, and although it creaked, it seemed to be fairly strong.

'Good enough,' I said. We checked the ladder was securely fixed onto the end of the last rope, and then pushed and shoved the whole mess to the edge of the well. I felt for the edge very carefully, lying down again and slowly dropping the whole loopy lot down into the void. I listened to it clatter downwards, praying it would be long enough, and that our knots would hold. Around me I could hear the spiders hissing and squeaking, and my skin crawled. I didn't know spiders made noises. Regan held tight to the top end of the rope, leaning back against the pull, letting the rope snake steadily. The ladder knocked against the well stones as we fed more rope and it dropped further. I was worried it would hit Lex on the head, so I yelled down, 'Watch out!'

Eventually I felt the pull of the hook, and I realised it was as far as we could go.

'Lex?' I called, feeling the edge of the well with my hands. 'Can you see the ladder? I need you to climb up.'

There was no answer.

'Lex?' I tried again.

'I can't,' came echoing back up. 'My ankle is dead where the phone hit it, and I'm so cold. I don't think my fingers will grip. I can't climb. I'm sorry.'

'What's she doing?' hissed Regan, and I blew out a breath.

'She can't climb up, so I think what I'm going to have to do is... go down, and tie her on.'

'**WHAT**?!' shrieked Regan. 'That's a terrible idea! Climb down there...? And how are you even going to get her up here...? And what would your *mum* say?' She sounded so outraged that I reached out and squeezed her shoulder.

'I'll... tie her onto the rope, and be able to help her climb up, for sure. And you guys can pull her

too. Use the hook and that long piece as a lever?'
I felt a shiver run up my back at the realisation
that I had to do this.

'Oh my God,' said Skylar, when she realised
that I was serious. I saw her rub her face hard.

'It'll be OK!' I said. 'But it's freezing down there
and Lex has been there so long already, we can't
leave her to go and get help. Plus... the outside
doors are jammed!'

'Your mum'll be back in about an hour,'
said Regan. 'Or... surely this situation is worth
smashing a window or two?'

'It'll take too long,' I said. 'We'd still have to
climb out and run somewhere for help, persuade
them it isn't a Halloween joke and then wait for
someone to come. If I go down, we'll have her out
by the time Mum's back, I promise.' I felt oddly
calm, and I rotated my shoulders before crawling
up to the edge again on all fours.

'Be careful, Bella, promise me?' said Regan. 'I
kind of like you... You know?'

'Yeah... me too,' said Skylar. 'You got me out of that chimney.'

I smiled at them in the dark, and somehow knew they were smiling back.

'We'll be right here watching, and we'll pull Lex up again,' Regan said, her voice only shaking a little.

'Right.' I cleared my throat and had another good look down the well. Then I got a tight hold of the cold, wet rope, and took a deep breath. I shifted onto my stomach and kicked my feet in first. I had a swoopy feeling as they hung out in the void, and it took me a moment of deep focus to start slithering down. 'Well... see you guys in a bit.'

I had to make myself breathe slowly to try and steady my thundering heart. My hands were shaking, but I forced them to grip until my knuckles burned. 'It's not that far down,' I said to myself as I swung lower. I faced the damp stones, focusing on the white spiders running up and around, scared to look down. Alice was right: it was just like descending into the very pits of hell.

After the awfulness of going over the edge, I quickly realised the stones in the well actually made good footholds, and even though the green stuff growing around them was stinky and slippery and I lost my toe grip a couple of times, I made it halfway down quite quickly. I tried to keep my face away from the arachnids and not to scream when a particularly big one crept past my nose or over one of my hands.

'No net,' I muttered to myself after skidding down a full metre. Above me Regan shrieked and the echo multiplied it until it was deafening. The rope had friction-burned my fingers and I took a minute to take my left hand off and blow gently on the pain.

'I'm coming, Lex,' I said, and tried to pinpoint how far down she was. 'Are you OK?' The closer I got, the more I could see her hair. It had turned as white as the spiders. I blinked and steadied myself at the horrible sight, trying to concentrate on the fact that the other effects had disappeared, and Lex's hair would go back to normal too. I swallowed hard.

'Just about,' she said after a long moment. 'Are you coming down that rope to hang with me?'

'I'm a-*frayed* knot,' I replied. The joke helped a tiny bit.

I realised it wasn't too much further, and got moving, hand over hand, as fast as I could. My arms burned, and I worked hard at ignoring my sore fingers. I tried not to think about climbing back up, with Lex next to me. *One thing at a time, Bella*, I told myself.

Then I heard a hiss.

29

'Was that you, Lex?' I asked in a falsely cheerful voice. As if Lex was hissing to keep herself warm or something.

'It's the spiders,' came the thin voice from below.

'Woah!' The rope swayed and I fought to steady myself. What was so bad about spiders? I tried to talk myself round. They were cute, right? *Little furry white... giant pincer mouth parts... creeping around in the dark... too many legs... OK. Think nice spider thoughts.* Did I know any spider jokes? My voice shook as I called down to Lex: 'How tall is a spider?'

'Stop with the jokes,' she said.

'About eight feet.'

'Are you trying to make me feel worse?' she answered, her voice echoing. 'Because there are a lot of spiders down here... you do know that... right?'

'I know...' I said, fighting to keep the panic from my voice. The rope creaked, and I held still, digging in my toes in case it was breaking.

After a long pause, Skylar called down to ask what was wrong.

'Nothing,' I called back up. 'Just hold that rope steady, OK?'

I got moving again, because my arms felt like rubber. The sooner I was down there, the sooner I could come back up. *Come on, Bella!* I told myself. *Come on! You don't want Mum to find you down here!*

I swallowed. *Excellent point*, I told myself. I pictured her face, all fierce at the top of the well. In my mind she looked distinctly furry, and spider-like. Nope. I shook my head again. *Concentrate!*

Down, down, down, lower and lower, until instead of vertical wall, my right foot touched down on horizontal stone. I pressed it about madly, not trusting what I was feeling, so when I turned around and saw Lex with the phone, the tiny light was as welcome to me as bright sunshine on a hot day. 'Yes!' I leaned and staggered across, grabbing her in a hug. I was thrilled that I'd reached her.

'I made it!' I yelled up to the duo, seeing that the cellar up there had shrunk into a tiny circle of grey at the top of the well. 'How deep is this?' I gasped as I took in the fact that Lex was standing on one leg, pale-faced, her hair strangely white and lank. She got hold of my arms and wouldn't let go.

'Oh my gosh, Lex! Are you... does it hurt?'

'Only my ankle,' she breathed. 'Where the phone hit. Luckily when it bounced I caught it.' She closed her eyes. 'I thought I'd die down here.'

'No, Lex,' I said in a loud voice. 'You aren't going to die. Come on, I'm going to tie you on and then help you climb.'

A huge, ghostly pale spider scurried over her foot and she didn't even wince but I let out a disgusted sound and backed away. As I looked closer, a massive one appeared from a tiny hole in the stone, squeezing through, followed by another equally leggy buddy. Their multiple eyes shone yellow in the little light, and when they hissed and raised their front legs I suddenly decided enough was enough.

'I don't want to get bitten. Look, Lex, have any of them bitten you?' I said shakily.

She shook her head. 'I'm so cold I can't feel my feet, but my trainers stayed on, thank goodness.'

Ugh. The very idea of having bare feet down here. My stomach heaved. Just being trapped alone down here was bad enough, but spiders... crawling all over you in the darkness, tickling your toes... no way.

'I have to tie you up,' I said, and grabbed Lex's hands. Her fingers were like sticks of ice. 'But we need to do the ladder bit first. Can you move closer at all?'

She wriggled and thrust up on her good leg, wobbling into my arms and crying.

'It's OK, I've got you,' I said. I hoped she'd be alright after all this. 'Happy Halloween,' I joked.

'I don't like Halloween any more,' she said.

'We agree about that, then.' I sized her up. 'I can give you a piggyback up?'

'Are you sure?' She blinked rapidly at me, and I jiggled the phone in my hand to check where the ladder was. It was about a metre off the bottom, a big jump up with her on my shoulders, but there was no other way. I swallowed my fear and grabbed her legs as she weakly tried to jump up. She felt cold and slimy, like a large frog. I wiped each of my hands on my jeans in turn and tried to get her feeling more secure.

'I have to turn the light out, to put the phone in my pocket – unless you can manage to hold it?' I said.

'Please, keep it on,' she begged. 'I'll hold it. Please.'

'OK, but do *not* drop it.' I realised the climbing would be easier if she had the light, because I could

245

see where to put my feet. I shook my hair back from my sweaty head. This was ultimate grossness.

'We're coming up!' I yelled up to Regan, who let down an echoing 'Whoop!'

I grinned. I could not wait to be back up there on solid ground. Just as I was setting my foot on the ladder, I heard Lex say, 'Wait.'

'What?' I asked, turning around clumsily with her on my shoulders. 'What's wrong?'

The air seemed to freeze around us, and Lex laid her head on my shoulder. 'It's just her,' she said, in a tired voice.

'Her who?' I asked, but I knew. 'Wait... is that Alice? In the *well*?'

'Don't leave me alone here,' Alice said, and I caught a wisp of silver, a pair of dark eyes. She was ghostly again down here, translucent and faint, but she frightened me. My hands gripped harder on the ladder.

'What do you mean?' I asked. 'Just float out, right?'

'There's something over there,' said Lex, and I felt her lean to the left. 'I think... she's trapped down here.' I hitched her up higher and shone the light around the bottom of the well. As I watched, the two closest spiders seemed to disappear. They *were* like the other creepies, the moths and the beetles.

'They aren't real,' I muttered. 'Now I've found you, they are vanishing. They're not real!' I felt like cheering, but I was too tired.

The light moved further around the well, and something caught my eye. In the corner was a small brown and white pile.

'What is that...?' I felt my heart skip as I examined the strange things. Deep inside, I knew what they were. I felt drained, like I was weighed down with an unbearable sadness. 'Oh no,' I whispered.

'Bones,' murmured Lex and Alice in one voice. The pile was roughly wrapped in brown material.

'Alice's pinafore,' I murmured in shock. 'Hold on,' I said, slipping Lex off my back. I knew what I had to do.

Gently, carefully, I lifted the bones, and tucked them into my hoodie. There didn't seem to be that many, and most were bound fairly tightly in the rotting material.

'It's OK, Alice,' I whispered.

When I had them all zipped safely inside, I lifted Lex again. They clicked gently together when I moved her into position. 'Time to go.'

I took a breath, and then another, and it was like the heavy sadness had lifted a little. The bones were hard and cold against my stomach, and they dug in as I gritted my teeth and jump-climbed the ladder. There was a heart-stopping moment when the top rung snapped, but I just swayed forwards and grabbed the rope like a professional climber. I bashed my forehead pretty hard, but I ignored the pain, digging my toes into two odd crevices and looping the end around Lex's stomach, under her arms and around. The ladder clattered down and I heard it break, but I told myself we didn't need it any more. Together we started to walk up the wall. As I moved I could see the large spiders fading away, and the vision gave me heart. The spiders were vanishing! No more big, pale, furry horrors. The light Lex held made it easier to see the right footholds, but I could also see the glistening stones and have time to be scared about how slippery they would be to climb on. I cupped one arm around her shoulders as best I could, but Skylar and Regan were doing the hard work, pulling Lex upwards. The rope creaked.

My fingers squeaked on the rope and I could feel blisters forming on top of my blisters. I clenched my teeth, feeling how Lex grew heavier with every step up. The footholds worked like a tiny, complex ladder. Steadily I climbed higher and higher, Lex breathing loudly in my ear.

'Come on!' yelled Regan. 'You're nearly halfway back; I can see the light!'

'You can do it!' Skylar chimed in.

I nodded and the rope wobbled. 'Stop nodding, idiot,' I growled, struggling now with every step. My arms and legs were shaking. 'Don't stop, you can't stop,' I chanted to myself. 'Up, up, up.' I pushed on and on, reaching and dragging, forcing us up with my toes. Everything ached and sweat prickled my skin and dripped into my eyes. I rubbed my forehead against the cold stone, and felt the sharp edges scrape my skin, hurting where I'd already bumped it. The pain woke me up a bit. *Keep going!* Regan's grip loosened and I realised she'd passed out or gone to sleep, so I stopped for a long moment and leaned into the wall again, using gravity to haul her further forward. I was terrified that she'd let go, so slowly and carefully I inched her arms beneath mine, and took the phone light back from her. After some consideration, I held it in my mouth.

'Come on!' shouted Regan, and I realised her voice was that much closer. But my arms were giving way. Everything was exhausted now, even my mouth. The phone was making me drool, and my teeth were throbbing, tired of clenching onto it.

At least we tried, I thought, as I felt my grip slipping. *At least we nearly did it. We nearly won the game.* Then my left hand let go.

'What are you doing!' howled Regan, leaning over and staring down at us. I gazed up at her and Skylar peering over. 'Don't you dare give up now! You've nearly done it!' She reached down an arm, and I saw how close she was. With a scream that made the phone vibrate painfully in my teeth, I forced myself to go up another few steps, and stretched up my arm. There was a bump as Skylar slid over backwards and the rope slipped. Our fingertips brushed for the briefest second, but I could go no further. I closed my eyes and took a sharp breath, ready to fall.

30

All of the strain disappeared as my screaming muscles quit at last. I had a horrifying feeling of lightness. No! We were going to die! I would kill Lex! It was all my fault – no!

Then the feeling of lifting again, but I knew it wasn't me who was doing it. We were gently going up, and then we were in Regan's arms, and Skylar was hauling us over the edge of the well. But the strangest thing was it felt like we were being pushed from beneath, rather than pulled from above. And then we collapsed on the cellar floor and Lex lay gripping on to my back, and Regan cried over us and hugged us, and I tried to catch my breath and wait for my body to come alive again.

My hands stung like I'd dipped them in a volcano, and I felt Skylar gently take her phone out of my clenched teeth and examine me with the phone torch.

'Not too awful,' she said, 'only a few toothmarks on the case. And you're OK too, of course.' But I could hear the wince in her voice as she shone her light on my hands.

'Skylar leaned right down and grabbed you and pulled you up, and then I could reach and I got your other arm just as you let go and we both did it!' Regan was waffling, patting my arm and sounding very relieved. 'And the spiders have all gone!' She twisted around to rapidly check the cellar floor, and then turned back to me, smiling and nodding. 'And Lex! Your hair looks cool!'

Lex blinked, touching her short hair with her hand.

I felt a tired smile creep over my face, the first proper smile it felt like I had smiled for a thousand years, and I knew that, somehow, working together had saved us. And then I unzipped my hoodie and with an enormous effort sat up, and tenderly laid out the bones next to me. Skylar shone the little light on them.

'What are those?' Regan's eyes were huge.

'We did it,' I said to them all. 'We found Lex and we found Alice.' I smiled again. 'We finished the game.'

'I always knew we would!' Regan whooped and grabbed us in another bear hug. I noticed we'd scooted close to the well edge again, so I pushed everyone back. Lex was sitting up now, a blank look in her eyes.

'Are you alright?' I asked her, and she nodded dreamily.

'Thank you,' she said, clasping my hand with surprising strength. 'You saved my life, all of you.' She blinked. 'I thought nobody would ever find me. I thought I'd never see light again.' She looked at us all in the little pool of light the phone torch made. Her hair shimmered silver, as pale as the spider bodies, before the old red colour started to return. 'It felt like... like she was draining all of my energy down there. I didn't want to die in the dark.'

'And you didn't. You're OK. We're all OK. Nobody here is ever going to die in the dark.' I was dithering, but I didn't care. What a night!

Then a figure appeared in the corner of the cellar, and we all stared up at it, too tired to feel much of anything. I noticed it was colder again. Alice.

'You won the game,' she said, and then she smiled.

I stared at her. Something was different.

'You found me, too,' she said. She looked at each of us. 'The game is finally over.'

Then there was a deafening roaring sound like a waterfall had hit us, and we clamped our hands over our ears, screaming in terror as Alice began to sway and shift in a strange silvery fog.

'Pa,' she said, facing the far cellar wall and holding out her hands. I stared at the space she was looking into, and slowly, the fog cleared. A tall man was there, holding arms out to her. He was weeping, and somehow I could feel his sorrow in my ribs, making them ache.

'Darling daughter,' he wept, his voice faint and echoing. 'I'm so very sorry. I hid myself in the trunk in my study, and I should have realised you'd eventually come seeking down here. I'm so sorry. But the door... it locked itself behind you. The key must have fallen out, and been lost. We never suspected you'd be here, at the bottom of that godforsaken well. The constable thought you'd run away... and we were searching the cities far and wide for a trace of you. Can you ever forgive me, daughter?'

Alice was sobbing too. 'Of course, Pa. I have missed you so much. I have waited for this day, this chance to finish the game.' She looked back at me for a second, and a ghost of a smile threaded her face. 'Lucky for me she was up to the challenge.'

'We did it together,' I said, clasping Skylar and Lex's hands. They both gripped Regan's.

Suddenly, as if from an immense distance came another figure, a woman. She wore a long skirt, and her hair was plaited and tied back.

She held her arms out to the weeping man, and to Alice, who stared at her in awe.

Then there was a blinding flash, and Alice was sucked down into the bones, twisting and fighting like a tiny whirlwind, bright white and full of strange energy. The noise faded and we sat up in awe to watch a long-dead thing whirl and knit itself back together, and the bones glowed blue-white for an instant before dulling down and returning to their soft cream colour. Everything went silent, and my ears popped after the crazy noise.

We looked at each other and stared at the sad little pile in silence. Alice was right: the game was over.

'Looks like everybody won,' said Regan after a moment. 'I think she's gone with her dad... and was that her mum?'

'I think it was,' said Lex. 'Wow.'

I stared at the bones. 'He'd tried to find her, but never checked down here. The door.' Something clicked in my head. 'That's why the doors here are weird: Alice got locked down here, so the people searching for her thought she couldn't have even entered the cellar.'

The others looked horrified.

'That door slammed on us too,' said Regan.

I nodded. 'She did all that, with the front door, and the cellar door when we came down.'

'What awful rotten luck.' Skylar shook her head. 'Just tragic.'

Everyone was silent.

'They have found each other now, though,' I said. My throat was burning and I coughed.

Then I tried to smile around at the girls in the cellar.

I paused. The *girls?* They were my *friends.* My chest seemed to swell and tears prickled the corners of my eyes.

'Alice helped, you know...' I said. 'I think she pushed us up, at the end there. I don't think I could have done it without her.'

Skylar snorted. 'Yes, you could, Bella. When you put your mind to it, you can do anything.'

We gathered together and had a group hug. Everyone seemed to be crying. Lex pulled my head down and kissed my cheek. 'Thank you, Bella. You're awesome.'

Then there was a huge rumble, and dust puffed out of the stone walls all around us.

'Maybe let's get out of here, OK?' said Skylar, looking around, an alarmed expression on her face.

'Before it's too late!' I yelled, as large stones started rumbling around us, almost like the whole floor was shaking apart. 'RUN!'

I screamed, as the wobbling and bouncing floor knocked me off my feet. Skylar thrust her hands over her mouth in shock. Lex held her arms out wide, staggering like she was dizzy, weaving around. 'Everyone come away from the well edge,' I said, grabbing her hand and hauling her away. The hanging rope snapped and snaked down into the dark hole. The edging stones of the well crumbled apart and fell down the well shaft, tumbling downwards and thudding as they piled up.

'We have to go!' I grabbed everyone's hands and we ran. 'The well! It's collapsing!' We started to run.

'The bones!' I panted, looking back, but it was too late. The well was crumbling inwards, and everything near the edge was falling in.

Jerking and stopping, we ran out of the cellar, dodging stones and bits of masonry that were jumbling up from the floor.

'Is the whole cellar collapsing?' shouted Skylar in my ear. I hoped not. I pictured Mum coming home to a mountain of rubble and my stomach swished like a washing machine. The ceiling appeared to be holding, along with the main stone walls. It was just the well, rumbling and collapsing in on itself like a dying star.

As we reached the foot of the steps, Lex screamed 'My ankle!', tripped over, and a rock hit her in the side of the head.

I crouched over her, helping her to sit up and checking she was OK. In the gloom I could see a patch of dark wetness, and I realised it was blood. Before I could panic too much, she shook herself like a cartoon character shaking off concussion stars and was up again, hopping and shouting 'GO!'

Behind us, the collapse sounded like the roaring of a hundred lions, and adrenaline flooded my tired muscles, making my feet fly. We ran faster than ever to catch up with the others, who were standing waiting to make their way up the stairs, beckoning us with their hands. It was confusing in the dark, but I realised we had a massive problem.

The staircase had been damaged by the

collapsing floor. The steps were on a crazy angle. Impossible and impassable.

'How are we going to get out of here?!' Regan coughed as Skylar whipped the little phone light around us to try and get our bearings. The dust swirling around made it harder to see.

I felt sick. Suddenly all of the massive effort to rescue Lex seemed to hit me at once. I swayed on my feet and Skylar shuffled to catch me.

'Bella!' she said in my ear. 'Are you OK?'

I tried to nod, but the little light flashing on the crumpled stairs was making me feel dizzy.

'Didn't you say there was another way out of here?' said Lex suddenly, still rubbing her head.

I blinked slowly. Yes, I was sure I'd seen something on one of the plans. Maybe not a way out, but something.

I started to move left of the stairs and leaned in to look hard at the far cellar wall. 'Bring the light!' I said, and Skylar followed me. The wall was stone, paved in an unusual criss-cross pattern.

We followed it all the way to the first corner of the cellar, the other two walking slowly after us, coughing in the dust. I pressed here and there, trying to figure out what the walls were supporting. This side was the least damaged as it was furthest from the well, but there were still disturbances and cracks in the floor. As I accidentally wedged my foot into one, I wondered what lay beneath the cellar. The underground stream that fed the well, but what else? Sewage pipes and rats' nests – I shuddered – plus lots of spiders. Then I remembered there were no white ghost spiders now. They had all vanished. I tried to cheer myself up, because as bad as this was, at least we weren't having to watch out for them.

'I can't see anything!' said Skylar, and Lex and Regan started thumping and pressing on parts of the brickwork. The dust was making my eyes water, and I rubbed them.

At the corner there was a massive wooden support, and I leaned on it, waiting for the others.

A cool breeze caressed my cheek, and I turned to it, letting it play over my sore eyes.

'Here,' said Skylar, passing me the phone. 'Something's different about that wall...' She bent down to check out some of the stones, but as I moved my arm back with her phone in my hand, my elbow hit part of the wooden support beam. There was another rumbling sound, and we all screamed. Was the ceiling falling in on us? I ducked down, and then watched in amazement as a narrow passageway opened before me, set right in the corner.

'Bella!' whooped Lex. 'You found a way out!'

'Is it safe?' I asked, as we all gathered at the hole, staring in.

'Let's go for it,' said Regan. 'What's the worst that can happen? Plus... we don't have a choice!'

I tried not to think of collapsing tunnels, bad air, suffocation or being crushed to death, and forced a smile.

We found each other's hands and held on

tightly, stepping in one after the other, our feet finding a tiny staircase in the gloom.

After about ten steps, the light on Skylar's phone went out, but we carried on in the darkness, the dusty air stinging and burning until it sounded like we were all choking.

'Ugh! Cobwebs!' spluttered Skylar, who was ripping through them first.

Last in line, I got a final glimpse of the cellar and saw how a huge pile of rubble and stones filled the void to the top as the well fell in on itself, everything in there shimmering behind a whirl of grey dust. 'Woah,' I breathed. The well was gone.

We held on tightly to each other, finally reaching a small wooden-floored area with cracks of light flooding through one of the walls. The floor creaked as we piled into the space, and Lex said 'Oof!' as I accidentally elbowed her in the stomach.

'Sorry!' I gasped. 'You're in the wars, aren't you!'

'Where are we now?' asked Skylar, running

her hands over the walls.

'Let's see!' said Lex, shoving forwards. She pressed her fingers along one of the strips of light and tried to squint through it, her nose right on the wood. 'I could be wrong, but I think we're behind the study bookshelves!' she said. I stared at her for a moment and nodded.

'That's right! It's not exactly a way out, but we found the secret passage!'

'Brilliant.' Regan folded her arms. 'So how do we get through it?'

My face fell. 'We have to... push everything again!'

Everyone went mad, shoving and pushing and thumping the inside of the bookcase to try and find out how to get out.

'I see something!' yelled Skylar, leaning forwards across my back where I was bending down.

'Ouch!' I said. 'Wait a minute, will you!'

She touched something and nodded. 'It's a tiny keyhole!'

'Where's the key?' yelled Lex and Regan together.

'Guys!' I said. 'Stand still a minute... did we knock it out?'

As one we all tried to bend down in the cramped space and bumped heads.

'Ouch! For goodness' sake, mine already hurts! What are your heads made of?' groaned Lex. 'Concrete?'

There was no key. We took it in turns to run our fingers around the dusty wooden floor, but the only thing I managed to find was a splinter. Great.

'We're locked in!' said Regan sadly. 'I don't want to be stuck here, behind a load of books!'

'Between a rock and a book-place,' said Lex.

I shoved my hands in my pockets glumly, and my fingers touched something sharp and cool.

My brain was whirring so hard to try and think of a way out that it took me a long minute to realise the answer was already in my hand. It was the tortoiseshell comb from the attic! I must have put it in my pocket instead of back into the tiny drawer. I slowly drew it out and grinned at the others.

'Watch this,' I said, and slid the top tooth of the comb into the lock. With a wiggle and a jiggle, and then a sharp karate chop downwards, something inside the lock clunked, and the whole wall swung open.

We stumbled out into the glorious light of the study, and then the wall of bookshelves clicked neatly back into place.

'Awesome!' said Lex, delighted. 'How did you do that, Bella?'

I looked mysterious and tapped my nose. I palmed the little comb and slipped it back into my pocket. I was going to keep it forever.

There was no sign of anything unusual, aside from our dusty footprints emerging impossibly from beneath the shelves. Regan pointed at them and giggled.

'They're kind of hard to explain!'

'It was just the well that fell in! Just the well!'

I squealed as I realised the rest of the house was still standing. I felt fuzziness wash over me, but this time it was pure relief. I'd been so worried that there had been massive damage up here, beyond the limits of the well and the cellar.

Everyone was smiling and clapping and hugging, and I was relieved to see that in the light, Lex's head didn't look too bad. We bumped fists and even started a few dance moves, until I heard a sound, and froze. Skylar realised what I was doing and hushed everyone else.

Just then, two things happened together. The old warped grandfather clock at the top of the stairs struck midnight, and the front door rattled.

32

We all ran through the parlour and froze into statues as Mum burst in. 'The front door obviously works fine now,' whispered Lex.

'It was just more of the weird stuff Alice did,' mouthed Skylar.

'Yes,' I whispered. 'The moths, beetles, even the spiders. A lot of creepy things, really, except for the well imploding... I think that *really* happened...' I tried to get a grip of myself.

Mum clattered in and dropped her bags at the bottom of the stairs, throwing her coat over the bannister. Then she turned around, fluffing out her hair, and jumped slightly when she saw us.

'Wow, guys! Great zombie make-up effects

for Halloween! You all look really convincing! Have you had fun?'

We nodded, and then I ran to her for a hug. 'I'm so glad you're home!' I said.

'Very glad to be home,' she answered, hugging me back.

We moved towards the lounge. I realised we all looked crazy – covered in soot and dust, streaked with cobwebs and grime. Lucky for us, Mum assumed we were in elaborate costumes. Then Regan let out a piercing scream, making us all jump violently.

'Oh God! What now!' I yelled as we turned to her, only to see Regan going bananas in the middle of the floor, shaking her head like a maniac.

'What's wrong?' shouted Lex.

'There's a spider in my hair!' she yelled, flipping about like she was in a frying pan.

A real one, I thought with a nod as Regan passionately flung the reassuringly normal black creepy-crawly over to the other side of the room.

'You lot had better go up to sleep soon,' said Mum, watching us with her head cocked to one side. 'Might I suggest a shower first, to save your sleeping bags from ruin? Some of you look a bit... tired?'

I nodded, ushering everyone to bed. 'Can I have a word please, Mum?'

'Has that girl hurt her ankle?' Mum said, after watching Skylar help Lex upstairs.

'Sort of,' I said.

She went into the kitchen to boil the kettle and I followed. This wasn't going to be easy.

'Goodness!' Mum stared around at the floor and the chimney.

'Ah, we were... excavating...' I said.

'You've uncovered some nice tiles.' She nodded. 'But why were you using the fish slice?'

'Erm, Mum.' I couldn't wait any longer. 'We... went in the cellar. And the well... collapsed.'

'You *what*?!' She shook her head. 'The well? Collapsed? Good grief.' She put a hand on her chest.

'My God. What if someone had fallen in?' She put her hands on her hips and frowned. 'Honestly, Bells, what on earth were you doing down there? I told you it was off-limits. I thought you'd be more sensible.'

I winced. 'It was sort of a Halloween game...'

I hid my hands behind my back so she wouldn't see my ragged fingernails and the blisters from clambering up the rope. 'Yeah, sorry, Mum. I forgot you'd said that. It could've been a nightmare.'

I stared at the floor, suddenly feeling so tired I could have fallen asleep on my feet. I didn't want to say anything else, but I knew I had to tell her everything.

'Actually, we did find something bad.' I looked at her, and she sat down, waiting for me to go on. 'Some remains. Bones.'

I nodded as her expression registered shock. 'Bella! Is this a Halloween joke?' she asked. 'Because it's not funny and it's not Halloween any more. It's All Saint's Day now, actually.'

'I'm not joking,' I said. 'I think they belonged to a girl who used to live in the house long ago.'

'Good grief!' she said, going pale. 'Who? What girl? What a night you all had. But I'm still cross with you, Bella.' She shook her head. 'It's a lot to take in...'

'I think she was called Alice Rose Monday,' I said. 'She went missing long ago, after she fell in the well. And she died here, in the cellar. Her father, the man who owned the house, didn't manage to... reach her. He was a vicar, called Solomon Monday.'

'Are you serious?' She shook her head, ignoring the boiling kettle. 'How do you know all of this?'

'Your research, actually. And Lex's – she did a project some time ago. For fun.'

I didn't tell Mum that Alice had told me most of it herself. I tried to look sorrowful.

She nodded and absent-mindedly tried to drink from an empty mug. She tutted and poured in a splash of milk. 'I suppose we'll have to call the police, and they'll have to examine where you found them.'

'They can't,' I said. 'The bones fell back down in the well, I think. It's a right state down there.'

'What!?' she barked, half-standing. 'Were you anywhere near it?'

'No. We were far back,' I said. It was bad to fib but she'd only worry herself. She didn't need to know the exact truth. In fact, I was trying hard to forget the exact truth.

'We'll still have to call the police. Tomorrow. Well, today, at a more reasonable time. Anyway, everyone's OK and safe... and I suppose your Halloween party thing ended up being... exciting. Hmm. I think that's it for you. No more parties, young lady.' She made herself some tea properly, pursing her lips.

I nodded. Fine with me.

'Now, go to bed. You look done in!'

I went up and had a shower to get the worst of the 'zombie make-up' off.

I grinned to see everyone had decided to share one room, Skylar and Regan joining Lex and me. We lay in a row on the floor, wrapped in our sleeping bags. It was heavenly to lie still and let my aching muscles rest, as everyone giggled and whispered. This was what it was really like to have friends, I thought, smiling up in the dark. Skylar leaned across and rubbed some expensive-smelling cream into my sore hands.

'She has really gone, hasn't she?' asked Regan, just as I was drifting off to sleep. I imagined the crazy roaring hurricane whirling back into the bones and shivered.

'Yep,' I said. 'Really.'

Morning came too soon, but at least it was the smell of bacon that woke us all up.

'Your mum's ace!' said Skylar as we piled downstairs, sniffing the scent like a pack of dogs.

The house looked different in the daylight, or maybe it was because Alice was gone. I hoped that wherever she was now, she had managed to find some peace.

Mum announced over coffee that the police were on their way.

'Do you need us to stay and talk to them?' asked Skylar, her mouth full of bacon and egg sandwich.

'No, love, Bella can fill them in with the details. There's no need to tie you all up in this. It might make the paper!'

'Ooh, I always wanted to be on the front page. Just give me a sec to blow-dry my eyelashes and I'll be picture-perfect,' said Regan, and I caught Lex's eye, glad to hear her sound so normal.

After a long lazy Saturday morning, Regan's mum came to pick the deadly duo up. They hugged Lex and I hard, and I wondered if it was actually fair to call them 'deadly'. Maybe their horrible experiences had made them nicer. Maybe not quite the 'delightful' duo, but close.

Then Skylar snapped at Lex for accidentally treading on her backpack and I shrugged. Maybe not.

After they'd gone, Lex and I had a hot chocolate and analysed everything hour by hour. 'In many ways, it was the most... terrifying Halloween party ever,' she said.

'A success, then...?'

We clinked mugs and I grinned.

33

The police were quiet and thorough, raising their eyebrows at the state of the collapsed well. Mum had called Bob, too, and he fitted some support poles just in case.

'Lucky you were nowhere near it,' said a tall inspector to me. They disappeared for a few hours and then another team in jumpsuits came back with some tools. After some careful digging, they found the bones and carefully transported them to a forensic anthropologist. Some weeks passed before we heard anything.

Mum and I worked on the house, but Lex also popped in a lot to help, and sometimes to sit and do homework. She was a real best friend. It was lovely.

Between us we figured out the secret passage and how to activate it from the library side. There was another tiny keyhole, and Mum had the keys. When we'd first moved here, Mrs Hallorann had sent her a big bunch, and half the trouble was figuring out which ones went where.

'It's a super feature,' Mum was saying. She loved the carved bed in the locked suite too, and the three of us polished up the nature engravings with honey-scented wax, until they gleamed like gold. I grinned to myself when I saw some moths, beetles and spiders all entwined in the design.

Mum got a letter saying the bones weren't identifiable. The police didn't have files going back that far, but there was a newspaper record of a girl called Alice Monday going missing. They concluded that she had died in Darkling Manor, but there was no way to determine whether it was an accident or something to do with Solomon Monday, her father, and the only other person who lived in the house at the time.

When I told Lex all this, she nodded solemnly. 'We'll never really know,' she said. 'But I think it was just a rotten accident. Alice played hide and seek, couldn't find her dad, decided to look in the cellar, fell into the well and badly injured her leg. Sadly, her poor father never suspected she was down there.'

We were silent for a long time, staring out of the window at the sky, watching the clouds race past. Was Alice up there now? I wondered. I hoped she was with her parents.

Mum and her team had almost finished the house, and from the cellar to the clock tower, everything was made safe and immaculate. I loved living in the houses when they were finished because it was like being rich. I sashayed around, padding on the thick carpets and running my fingers through the amazing curtain tassels. In the garden, Mum had replaced one key stained-glass window and set in some subtle spotlights around the chapel ruin so it could be admired.

I squinted and saw it as Alice had shown me, a beautiful chapel where her father had worked and brought comfort to the community.

One Sunday morning, I passed the entrance to the cellar, now replaced with a rich oak-panelled door. There was a strange whooshing sound, like a wind blowing, and I paused to listen. It could have been the old house moving or creaking, but I could have sworn I heard a girl's voice giggling. 'Coming ready or not!' The hairs on the back of my neck stood on end. I shook my head rapidly as if to clear my ears and ran up the stairs to my room.

That night at dinner, Mum announced Mrs Hallorann was coming. She rested her chin in her hands as she watched me eat.

'Look, love,' she said, and I froze. It was what she always said when it was time to move on. To start over again.

'This has been a difficult house for you, I know. Finding those bones... well, I guess

I'm lucky you are still OK, not needing counselling or anything.'

I stared down at my spaghetti.

'So we'll be off soon, right, love?' She patted my hand.

Suddenly I lost my appetite and pushed my plate away. There was no point arguing, no point saying, *Can't it be different this time? Can't we stay, for once?*

'I'm not hungry.' I went upstairs to my room and stared out at the neat front garden. Stupid girl, I was. Why did I expect my life would be any different just because I had made a friend?

Mum tapped on the door and came in. 'What's wrong, Bella?'

'It's just... I like Lex, you know. I was starting to feel, sort of... normal. Even the deadly duo aren't really deadly now.'

She looked puzzled. 'The who?'

'Never mind.' I sighed.

'I'm sorry, Bells.' She gazed at me sadly. 'Maybe you and Lex can be pen pals?'

I shook my head. How lame.

The door knocker banged, and Mum straightened up. 'That'll be Dolores,' she said. 'We'll talk more later.'

Mrs Hallorann and Mum took ages to go over the whole house, and I could hear her American voice getting louder and more excited. I smiled for Mum, because obviously the woman loved what Bright Interiors had done to the place.

Then they tapped the door and came in, so I sat up and smiled.

'Dolores, I don't know if you remember Bella, my daughter?'

'Aw, of course I do. What a doll!' Mrs Hallorann ran towards me and grabbed my hand. I tried not to stare at her skinny ostrich legs. 'You've done a tremendous job here, I can't tell you. Your mother here is my new favourite person, and she tells me you had the police here, and you had bones in the cellar! And she was so worried, my girl, can you believe it? As if I, a property magnate, would be worried about a few little bones. No siree. In fact, I kinda got the idea to market this place as a haunted hotel, do y'hear me? I'll rake it in!' She leaned out of the window and sucked in air through her nostrils. 'And the secret passage! I know folks from Carolina to Canada who just adore that stuff!'

She leaned out of the window, breathing in deeply.

'It's just so delicious here, I can't believe it. You guys are so lucky! I think I can even smell the rain! I love your English weather – it's so wet and fresh and different to what we get in the States. You're just so amazingly green. I love it! Little apple trees! Just like a storybook.'

I caught Mum's eye and we tried not to laugh.

'So, tell me, where are you guys off to next?' she said, and Mum just shrugged.

'I think we'll go south for a change. Maybe find a beachfront property to work on.'

I tried to energetically focus on the fact we

would be going to live at the seaside, but I could only see Lex's face.

Mrs Hallorann nodded thoughtfully and grabbed hold of Mum. 'Come with me, Julie. Let's walk and talk.'

They talked for another hour downstairs, and I heard them both laughing. I tried to write a goodbye letter to Lex, but I kept screwing it up. In the end I lay on my bed and let the tears flow. Maybe I was meant to be lonely. Maybe I was just a girl who wasn't ever meant to have a best friend.

More time passed and I realised I was starving. I headed to the top of the stairs to see if I could sneak some toast, and saw Mrs Hallorann leaving.

'So long, Julie!' she was yelling. 'Thank you for everything! I'll have the contract emailed to you from New York!'

Jam or marmalade, I was thinking. *Maybe a hot chocolate with cream to cheer myself up?*

Then Mum came bounding up to meet me.

'Well, Bella, I have some news for you. Dolores has made me an offer!'

'What?' I blinked. Mum looked like a schoolgirl.

'How would you like to stay right here, in Castleton?' she asked, her eyes shining.

I grabbed her hands. 'Are you serious?!' I gasped.

'Yes! Dolores wants to work on developing the damaged cellar into a subterranean spa, which would be another year's work at least. And then there's a second large project, a local manor house. So guess what? She's offered us a cottage! Just a few streets away, actually!'

'So I can stay at the same school?' I asked, not daring to believe what I was hearing.

'Yes!'

'That's wonderful!' I screamed, leaping up and whirling her around and dancing a dangerous jig out onto the landing. 'A cottage?'

'Steady!' she yelled, dancing too. 'Dolores bought it in an auction, and it's a mess. So much work!' Mum clenched her fists in excitement. 'We can showcase our gargoyles, and our skills. She doesn't really need it, so she's offered to sell it to me at a very reasonable price.'

'So we'd stay there for *ever*?' My eyes felt huge in my face.

'Yes,' said Mum in a quieter voice, drawing me into a hug. 'Forever, Bells, if you wanted to.'

'Our first real home!' I shouted, poised to run back to my room and text Lex.

ACKNOWLEDGEMENTS

There are so many people to thank for helping me to write this book. I couldn't have done it without them.

Firstly, my fabulous agent Thérèse Coen. She plucked this story from the slush pile and gave me this wonderful opportunity, for which I thank her and the whole team at Susanna Lea Associates so very much.

To my publisher extraordinaire, Felicity Alexander, marketing and publicity gurus, Susan Barry, Emily Finn, Sarah Farmer and the brilliant people at Welbeck Flame, thank you from the bottom of my heart for choosing Bella Bright. Your support has afforded me an utterly amazing and life-changing opportunity.

The delightfully creepy cover and illustrations are all down to the incredibly talented Beatriz Castro and I'll never forget how magical it was to see Bella for the first time. I couldn't breathe!

A special enormous thank you to author Emma Finlayson-Palmer, who believed in me and my writing and has continually supported and inspired me over the years.

To my beta readers and writer friends – genius authors Jenny Pearson, Tess James-Mackey, and Lis Jardine; the whole '23 debut group, and Stuart, Melissa, Florianne, Emily and Sophia; the gang at Write Mentor– thank you all so much.

To my own BFFs Laura Moss and Bernie Lanaway – thank you too for your continued support and encouragement. Jo, Ashley, Helen, and Amarjit (CCW!) Gill, Rob, Mossy, Des, and Hudson too – thank you guys.

To my wolf pack – there are too many of you to mention and you are ALL brilliant but special thanks must go to Shell H, Shell OD, Ryan, and the Saturday Squad-Chloe W, Luke, Gem, Arjun, and Phoebe, who have been so supportive. Love to all of you!!

John Ward Snr, and Sarah and Scott Pedder, I've always appreciated your kind words to keep at it. Thank you! In memory of my remarkable mother-in-law, Margaret Ward, who always believed I could do this. She is greatly missed.

To my amazing sisters Charlotte Ward and Chloe Harrison – thank you for being magnificent through some very tough times. Your families are wonderful and we have all leaned together and got through. Thanks Richard Ward and Nic Harrison, his lovely mum Di, and of course my nieces and nephews Harry, Isobel, Phoebe, Caelan and Seth.

To Mum – thank you for being so brilliant, and so strong and tough! You're incredible.

To my darling John and our star-babies - Jess, JJ and Ethan. Thank you for being totally awesome. You inspire me every day; I'm very lucky to have you.

If you are ever in or around the West Midlands – you may have time to visit any of these amazing places which helped to inspire elements in the novel:

· WILD Zoological Park, Halfpenny Green
· Dudley Zoo
· The Butterfly Sanctuary, Stratford
· West Midlands Safari Park, Kidderminster

And discover ghosts of the past at:

· Bantock House, Bantock Park, Wolverhampton

· The Victorian Glasshouse, West Park, Wolverhampton

· The Black Country Living Museum, Dudley

· Wightwick Manor, Tettenhall

RESOURCES:

Action For Stammering Children has lots of wonderful information on their website if anyone is interested to find out more, or wants help and support.

https://actionforstammeringchildren.org/

ABOUT THE AUTHOR

Carolyn Ward studied for an English degree in Wolverhampton before moving to Manchester, where she rode horses around Manchester City's training ground and nearly fell in the river. Now settled in South Staffordshire and mum to three, she writes MG horror. In her spare time she enjoys shopping for haunted antiques and unusual tarot cards. Bella Bright is her debut novel.

Twitter: @Viking_Ma

Facebook: https://www.facebook.com/CarolynWard101

Instagram: @carolynwardwriting

TikTok: @carolynwardviking

Website: https://carolynwardwrites.wordpress.com/

ABOUT THE ILLUSTRATOR

Beatriz Castro was born in Logroño, La Rioja, Spain. When she was a little girl, she was always drawing and writing fantastic stories. She studied at the school of arts in her native town, Logroño. After graduating in Illustration from there in 2008, she embarked on a career as a professional illustrator. Her books have been published by numerous international publishing houses. She likes animals and books, classic stories and fairy tales and listens to rock and punk music. Beatriz is the illustrator of the Nevermoor series.

Instagram: @beatrizcastroilustradora

Website: http://beatrizcastroilustracion.com